NORSE MYTHOLOGY

Learn about Viking History,

Myths, Norse Gods, and Legends

AMY HUGHES

TABLE OF CONTENTS

INTRODUCTION TO NORSE MYTHOLOGY

This is an in-depth introduction to Scandinavian mythology, including the pagan setting and the characteristics of the Viking people, necessary to better understand the birth of the myths and legends of the North.

The Valkyries, the wise Odin, the mighty Thor, and the enigmatic Loki, before becoming icons of certain films, were the protagonists of an extraordinary world from which artists—from Wagner to Quorthon, from Robert E. Howard to Tolkien—of every era have drawn heavily. These heroes move within a cosmology of extraordinary complexity supported by Yggdrasil, the ash of the world whose trunk crosses all nine existing worlds, an evergreen symbol of the eternal flow of life through various levels of existence, a powerful plant metaphor that unites heaven and earth in an inescapable destiny.

Before we start, it is useful to note that, unlike Judaism, Christianity, and Islam, Norse mythology is not a revealed religion: These stories were not transmitted directly to us by a superior entity. Rather, they are the fruits of the hand of man.

Curiously, these stories and testimonies do not come from pagan writers but, rather, from Christian monks who managed to wrest them from oblivion. These myths, which make up the traditional religion of the Scandinavian peoples before their Christianization, were, in fact, transmitted orally. The act of engraving runes on stone, wood, or metal, as happened among the Vikings, was difficult to reconcile with long and detailed stories like those of pagan heroes. It will be necessary to wait for the arrival of Christianity, which, together with the crosses, also spread the art of writing with a pen. However, there was a compact tradition of legends and stories that was transmitted from generation to generation by the bards, who recited long poems and adventures concerning the Gods.

The fundamental text for understanding Norse mythology is the Edda, written by Snorri Sturluson around 1220. A man of many talents, Snorri draws very carefully from pagan sources, managing to preserve the religious heritage of his people and to not alter it with Christian morality. Snorri, in fact, describes the deeds of the Nordic deities by rejecting the evil and demonic image in which they appeared in the descriptions of some Christian preachers.

To explain the nature of Norse mythology, we must briefly analyze the history of paganism in northwestern Europe.

During the Roman Empire, the various barbarian tribes (especially Germanic) lived on the borders of the Empire, which, despite exerting obvious influence on them, failed to significantly affect their language and beliefs. When the Empire began to collapse, between the fourth and sixth centuries after Christ, the various tribes began to conquer the lands no longer under control of the Roman army.

The old kingdoms were dismembered and, over the years, great powers were formed, such as Anglo-Saxon England and Merovingian France.

Christianity spread quickly, from the center to the outside, and most European peoples denied the old Gods in favor of the religion of the Book.

Between the tenth and eleventh centuries after Christ, the Norwegian people were converted by two kings: Olaf Tryggvason and Olaf the Holy. Their dominion was characterized by bloody persecutions of the pagans: Their temples were burned, their idols destroyed, the followers persecuted and killed. Some of them managed to save themselves by fleeing to Iceland, a kingdom without kings and without persecutions but that pagan fire, after a last vital spark, died down a few years later.

Denmark also succumbed to the missionaries, quickly becoming a pillar of the Church.

For a moment, the Swedes succeeded in preserving their traditions but in 1164 the ecclesiastical power penetrated and conquered even Uppsala—the largest Swedish pagan center and the city that, in the collective imagination, was the legendary stronghold of Odin and Freyr.

Before the fairly widespread diffusion of Christianity, however, the North venerated its Gods for more than a thousand years and, at the end of Scandinavian paganism, the Vikings from Norway and Sweden were the terror and scourge of Europe. During this long period of time, paganism was able to be shaped and broken down into different forms and rituals, as there was neither a universal faith nor written sacred texts. The Scandinavian pantheon was, in fact, influenced by the paganism of the Mediterranean and of Eastern Europe and by the Christian Church itself. The faithful lived a very personal and varied religiosity, with strong differences according to the places and times where it was lived.

By "a Nordic pantheon," we mean a fairly homogeneous set of cultures which, from a period dating from around the third millennium before Christ to the establishment of Christianity, preserved many common features, in a vast territory that includes Northern Europe, the Balkans, Germany, and Scandinavia.

It is interesting to note, in fact, that some common features among religions before the Book are still reflected in our everyday lives. Týr the cripple, the tutelary deity of the right victory in the battle for the Vikings, at the time of the formation of the names of the Northern week, became the God of War, identified by the Romans as Mars. The English "Tuesday" is none other than the Northern equivalent of Tuesday, the day consecrated to the bellicose God Mars. Thursday (in Norwegian "Torsdag") derives from the God of Storms, Thor. The great diffusion of his cult led to the translation of the name of the day dedicated to him as Dies Jovis, thus attributing to him the same importance of our Jupiter. And what about Friday (in Norwegian "Fredag"), which refers to the Goddess of Fertility, Frigg—so similar to "our" Venus?

To try to understand Norse mythology, we need to briefly describe the Vikings, whose stories of looting in France, Germany, Spain, and England filled the Christians with terror. The ecclesiastical chroniclers of the time, frightened by the violence and fury of the men of the North, came to portray them as the instrument with which God punished men, angry for their sin.

However, the image in the collective imagination of the "northern devils" is due not only to the bloodshed that characterized their incursions but also to the high frequency with which such raids took place. The Vikings raided much more frequently than did other populations but not for "simple" bloodlust. Living mainly on the Scandinavian islands and coasts, they did not have many ways to expand their territories to cope with a growth in population. The raid, therefore, had a double purpose: to settle in more favorable territories and to obtain resources otherwise difficult to find in Scandinavia. Initially, the Vikings returned to their settlements after the looting but, later, they started to establish rich commercial outposts in the areas where raids took place more frequently, such as England and Ireland. For example, in the ninth century, the Norwegian Vikings settled permanently in Ireland, where they founded the current Dublin, which from a simple settlement soon became a large and prosperous city. Their rule in this area, however, lasted only a few years, as they were driven out by an alliance of Irish and Danes. The latter, unlike their Swedish and Norwegian brothers, had already begun to organize themselves into a real kingdom to form a united front against the Carolingian Empire, which was beginning to become a dangerous enemy.

Thus, France, England, Germany, the Baltic countries, and Spain simply had the misfortune of being the territories closest to the Vikings, soon becoming their favorite targets.

Ironically, this predilection remains alive today, as evidenced by the many hordes of Norwegian elders who settle in Spain to enjoy their retirement. However, the Vikings cannot be labeled simply as bloody barbarians. Undoubtedly, they managed to be brutal (so they must certainly have appeared to the inhabitants of the cities that had the misfortune of being subjected to their incursions). However, in reality, though forged in a hostile context, the Viking culture is much less crude than we think. Their leaders were often men of culture and common sense: They loved art and hero stories and revered their large longships and their swords, both for their beauty and for their usefulness in battle. They were also great traders, with a keen spirit of organization. Many of them built large commercial networks and were considered wise and worthy members of the communities with which they traded. They were courageous and, despite their strong individualistic character, they were loyal to their leaders. They opposed any attempt to limit their freedom but they were also capable of great discipline. A man, whether friend or foe, who was ready to die for what he considered important was held in high esteem and was even more admired if he died on the battlefield with a smile on his lips and the gross hands of the blood of the enemies.

These behaviors are reflected in the recurring motifs of Norse mythology, in which the threat of the forces of Evil is frequent in a context in which war inevitably reigns. The figure of the Norse hero is, therefore, that of a great warrior, capable of enduring formidable exploits but unable to escape death. For the Vikings, nothing was eternal and when the fate of the Gods was fulfilled, the end of all things would come. In fact, the Norse Gods, unlike the Greek and Roman ones, were not immortal. According to Norse mythology, at the end of time, there would be a great battle: Ragnarök, in which most of the Gods would die and the world would be destroyed, only to rise from its ashes.

But that is another story…

CHAPTER 1: VIKING ORIGINS

More or less between 800 AD and 1100 AD, the Vikings left their lands—Scandinavia and Denmark—in search of fortune. The Vikings were quick and agile sailors and warriors, pirates who could surprise their enemies in very effective ways, which were enriched by raiding coastal settlements—particularly the monasteries of the British Isles.

During the next three centuries, the Vikings became merchants and settlers. Some of them would enter the European powers' game, and all would leave their mark across Europe, in Russia, in Iceland, in Greenland, and going as far as Terranova, in the American continent.

The name "Viking" derives from the ancient Norse language. It did not refer to a people but to an occupation. The term derives from the word "vik" (bay or inlet) as a testament to the maritime vocation of these people. According to another hypothesis, the name derives from the word "vikja," which meant getting away and moving. We do not know precisely why the Vikings left their land; surely, they were in search of fortune and loot, probably because there had been a strong demographic increase. What we do know is that their boats, the Drakkar, were extremely fast and maneuverable.

The Norse language was a Germanic language, just like English and German. Even the Germanic peoples who had already lived in Europe for centuries, such as the Franks, the Saxons, and the Lombards, had most likely arrived from Scandinavia and, just like the Vikings, had worshiped deities like Odin. In the ninth century AD, however, the Vikings were perceived as pagan, ferocious, and dangerous people.

The term "Viking" simply indicated men dedicated to pillaging by sea, and for this reason they did not have a particular ethnic identity. They could be Danes, Norwegians, or sometimes even Lapps. The main differences between the Vikings and those who already lived in Central and Southern Europe were more than cultural: The Vikings were foreign to the "civilized" culture of the Romanized and Christianized Germanic peoples. During the eighth century, the Vikings had already interacted with them through trade, especially fur. When the Vikings reached continental Europe, they knew it was inhabited by populations at war with each other, and in possession of many treasures to raid.

In 793, the Vikings attacked Lindisfarne, a sacred island located on the Northumberland coast, in north-eastern England, which housed a very important monastery. This date also marks the full rightful entry of the Vikings into European history. It is the first Viking attack described in a chronicle.

Those who attacked Lindisfarne had probably been Vikings from Norway. The monastery was not destroyed but the behavior of these pagan Vikings created a very strong impression because, until then, monasteries of this type had always been respected. That is why, among other things, they were not supervised in a particular way.

Two years later, there were new attacks by the Vikings on other defenseless monasteries on the Hebrides and in Ireland. In 799, there was the first attack in continental Europe, at the monastery of San Filiberto in Noirmoutier. For many years, the Vikings would continue to raid key points in the British archipelago (particularly in Ireland) and in Europe, also focusing on important points of trade such as Dorestad, 80 km from the North Sea, particularly targeted starting from 830.

After the death of the Carolingian emperor Ludovico the Pious, the Vikings began to intervene in the civil war between the heirs to the Carolingian throne when one of them, Emperor Lotario I, asked the Vikings for help against their brothers. However, the Vikings didn't begin to settle in Europe until the ninth century.

In the mid-ninth century, the Norwegian Vikings began to settle in Ireland, Scotland, and England. They established cities like Dublin, Waterford, and Limerick on the Irish coast. These were bases for raids on England and inland Ireland as well as on important exchange centers. The Vikings also controlled large portions of northern Scotland and its islands: the Shetlands, the Orkneys, and the Hebrides.

Since 865, the Danes, with a real army, had been trying to conquer and colonize the whole of England. The Anglo-Saxon chronicles in 865 remember it as the Great Danish Army, a veritable horde of pagans who, at the end of the ninth century, managed to conquer most of England.

The England of that time was divided into seven Anglo-Saxon kingdoms: a balance undermined by the Danes, who, in a few years, conquered East Anglia (870) and Northumbria (867) and dismembered Mercia. The only kingdom capable of facing them through an effective system of fortifications (defeating them even in battle in 871) remained Wessex, in the southernmost part of the island. The Danish army therefore settled further north, in the kingdom of Northumbria, making the city of York an important center of trade and mingling with the subject populations.

Towards the middle of the tenth century, the reign of Wessex, a bastion of Anglo-Saxon resistance, managed to reconquer most of the areas dominated by the Scandinavians, bringing England together under a single crown and finally driving away King Eric (nicknamed "Bloody Ax") from Northumbria. As we will see later, however, the Vikings would soon be back.

Parallel to the conquests in the British archipelago, other Vikings settled on the European continent, where, more or less from the tenth century, they were known as Normans. In addition to coastal cities like Nantes (sacked in 842), they reached the hinterland, plundering cities like Paris, Orleans, and Tours. In Spain, they besiege Seville (then owned by the Arabs) in 844, while in Italy, in 859, they went as far as Pisa.

These Vikings succeeded in obtaining a land concession in 911 from the king of the Western Franks, Charles the Simple, for the first time in history. It was a piece of Neustria, exactly the city of Rouen, in France, with the surrounding territories. In exchange for this, their leader Hrolfr (also known as Rollone in Italian) undertook to protect the passage of the Seine, in particular by blocking access to other Vikings. Rollone was baptized the following year and obtained the position of Count of Rouen. The territories under its control took the name of Normandy, which they still preserve today.

After the year 1000, some of these Normans belonging to the Altavilla family arrived in southern Italy, conquering lands in Capua and Melfi. In 1059, Robert Guiscard was to become Duke of Puglia and Calabria, while his brother, Roger I, would conquer Sicily, taking it from the Arabs. In 1130, Roger II—Roberto's nephew and son of Ruggero I—was crowned King of Sicily, bringing together Norman Southern Italy under a single crown.

Also in the ninth century, the Norwegian Vikings had begun to colonize Iceland, an island that was then almost completely uninhabited. An Icelandic saga preserved in manuscripts of the fourteenth and fifteenth centuries tells us that at the end of the tenth century, from Iceland, the Vikings reached Greenland. Among them was the famous Erik the Red, whose son, Leif Eriksson, around the year 1000, managed to reach Terranova. The new lands were named "Vinland" (land of wine) by the Vikings.

To confirm the veracity of the sagas, in 1960 in Terranova, near Anse aux Meadows, the remains of a Viking settlement were found. It is not known whether it is the legendary Vinland described by the sagas but it is certain that between the tenth and eleventh centuries, the settlement was inhabited (it seems for only three years) by Vikings.

Other Norse-speaking Scandinavian warriors and pirates, apparently from present-day Sweden, had instead gone eastwards, reaching the Slavic countries and then Byzantium, where they were called variaghi. The history of the variaghi is very different from that of their Viking "colleagues" because, rather than raiders and territorial lords, they soon became merchants and mercenaries. Nevertheless, they attacked Constantinople (in 860 and 941) and even Persia. It seems that from these populations, called Rus by the Slavic sources, came Novgorod and Kiev—two states from which Russia originated. This is, however, a very debated position and, therefore, uncertain.

Also around the middle of the tenth century, King Aroldo II, known as Azure Teeth, converted to Christianity and succeeded in unifying Denmark and Norway. Thus began a new age for the Vikings, who returned to their ancient sights on England. Sweyn Barbaforcuta, rebel son of Aroldo, succeeded in conquering it in 1013, exiling King Etelredo II. His son Canute the Great (Knut) came to reign over a real empire, which included England, Denmark, and Norway.

England was reconquered by the Anglo-Saxons in 1042, with Edward the Confessor, who was to be followed in 1066 by the last Anglo-Saxon king of England, Aroldo II. Aroldo II reigned for less than a year, during which he defended England from another Viking invasion, this time headed by King Harald III of Norway. Meanwhile, the Duke of Normandy, William, a powerful feudal lord of the King of France, had thought about taking advantage of the situation by invading England.

On October 14, 1066, with the Battle of Hastings, the Normans definitively defeated the Anglo-Saxons, killing King Aroldo II. The crown of England then passed to William I the Conqueror, Duke of Normandy, in a sense, therefore, a descendant of the Vikings. From that moment on, English history was closely linked to French history: The King of England was also the Duke of Normandy and, consequently, a vassal of the King of France.

But the times of the Viking raids were long gone. Already with Aroldo II, the Scandinavian kingdoms had become Christian kingdoms, perfectly inserted in medieval Europe. As for the culture of the Vikings, it had been absorbed by the European and Christian culture, surviving in the Icelandic sagas as well as in the toponyms of many places in Europe.

The Temple of Uppsala

There are many and varied testimonies that remain of what was the pagan religion in the Viking era when no Christian had yet dared to venture into the northern lands overflowing with ancient sagas of brave warriors ready to prove their worth by challenging fearsome creatures.

Uppsala, the last great pagan temple, was destroyed with the Christianization of the country in the eleventh century but it certainly represents one of the most significant testimonies of the religious traditions in use among the northern peoples of modern Scandinavia as well as in Iceland and Denmark.

The archaeological site that includes the religious structure can be considered one of the central places of the period of interest, including, in addition to the numerous mounds, several places used for diverse tasks such as schools and economic centers.

A testimony of this we again find in the connection between law and religion. In fact, in ancient cultures, war was accompanied by some rituals that served, beyond guaranteeing the success of the battle, to also confer prestige to the sovereign and his rank.

In this temple, decorated entirely in gold, people worshipped the statues of three Gods in such a way that the most powerful of them, Thor, occupied a throne in the center of the chamber. Odin and Freyr were placed at Thor's sides.

The role of these Gods was as follows. Thor, it is said, presided over the air, which governs thunder and lightning, wind and rain, good weather and crops. The other, Odin, administered the war and gave man the strength to fight his enemies. The third is Freyr, who gave peace and pleasure to mortals.

Near this temple was a large tree with several branches, green in both winter and summer. No one knows what species it belonged to. There was also a well in which the pagans usually made their sacrifices, and a man sometimes threw himself into them. If the sacrifice failed to return to the surface, the desire of the people would be granted.

A gold chain ran around the temple. It hung from the tympanum (architectural structure) of the building and sent its sparkle from afar to those approaching because the sanctuary was on a flat surface, with mountains in perspective, like in a theater.

The priests had the task of offering sacrifices in the name of the people. If plague and hunger threatened their lands, an offer was paid for the idol Thor. If war raged, for Odin. If weddings were celebrated, for Freyr.

It was customary at Uppsala to hold a general feast of all the provinces of Sweden at nine-year intervals. No one was exempt from participating. Kings and everyone had to send their gifts to Uppsala. The extent of the sacrifice happened as follows: For every male living being, they offered nine heads with the blood necessary to appease the Gods. The bodies were hung in the sacred wood that bordered the temple.

Feasts and sacrifices of this kind were celebrated for nine days. Every day they offered a man with other living beings in such numbers that seventy-two creatures would be offered over the nine days. This sacrifice lasted about the time of the spring equinox.

However, archaeologists seem to be discussing, above all, the very nature of the building—that is to say, whether it was a temple or something different.

One aspect of the rituals held in Uppsala that is almost completely ignored by these reporters, except for Snorri, is that a cult of the Goddesses also took place in conjunction with the assembly of the Gods.

In fact, this ceremony played a central role and was called "Dísablót," which literally means "sacrifice for the Goddesses" that some think are the three Nornir: Urðr, Verðandi, and Skuld.

Most historians believe that this ritual performed by the "blótgydja"—that is, a sacrificial priestess—was intended to improve the next harvest in which the various cults linked to the productivity of the land were reflected.

In Sweden, the Dísablót was of great political and social importance. However, the sources focus on the three divinities stated above and on the barbarous nature of sacrifice, leaving out this custom.

It should be kept in mind that most of the writers of that period were Christians and could not tell traditions, to which they were strangers, better than those who wrote those myths, sagas, and other works that came to us.

Nonetheless, by combining the various sources, it is possible to see that the Uppsala Temple could also have been an attempt to copy, in real life, the mythical concept of a divine parliament whose unknown forces held the laws of the cosmos.

The Blood Eagle

As much as the Vikings loved to plunder and kill during their raiding, they informed Norse peoples only as brutal and unscrupulous warriors who did nothing but exclude a large portion of their daily lives, an often more fascinating aspect of the heroic war of legendary warriors.

Until the nineteenth century and for most of the twentieth century, the dominant image of the Viking world was almost represented by an exaggeration of their brutality and their fighting spirit—a picture that contributed to the birth of some myths that still persist as a reality of the Norse world.

True, the Vikings killed, looted, and enslaved at the first available opportunity but they were much more than cruel war animals.

One of the most persistent Viking myths is that of the blood eagle, a method of execution involving an extremely violent and brutal death.

According to the Norse sagas, King Aelle of Northumbria was one of the most illustrious victims of the blood eagle, a procedure that took place in distinct phases:

The prisoner was tied up and made to lie down with his face towards the ground;

An eagle with extended wings was probably engraved on the prisoner's back, likely with a scramasax;

The ribs were then separated from the spine by ax strokes, one by one;

The ribs and skin were pulled outwards to form a pair of "wings" on the back of the condemned;

Handfuls of salt were thrown on the living flesh to increase pain (according to the two historians, the condemned man was still alive and conscious at this stage);

The lungs were extracted and placed on the "wings."

Considering the most brutal aspects of Norse life (including human sacrifices for religious purposes), this method of execution was considered not only credible but also relatively common, especially as a ritual sacrifice, by many historians of the past.

The blood eagle seems to have been practiced also on Halvdan Hålegg of Norway, on the Irish sovereign Máel Gualae, and on a couple of legendary figures like the giant Brusi. However, the most famous and historically most relevant execution is probably that of King Aelle of Northumbria.

The brutal execution of King Aelle seems to be linked to the vengeance of Ivar Ragnarsson, the Boneless, to avenge the murder of his father, the legendary Ragnar Lothbrok, thrown into a pit full of poisonous snakes by order of the ruler of Northumbria.

There are no written testimonies of the contemporary blood eagle to the period of the executions of Halfdàn, Máel Gualae, or King Aelle but only sources compiled at least 150 years after these events.

Almost all the sources that gave rise to the history of the blood eagle are also skaldic poems known to be cryptic, rich in metaphors related to Norse mythology, and difficult to interpret if decontextualized or fragmented.

It is more likely, instead, that the blood eagle (at least the procedure described above, which has entered the collective imagination) is a myth born from the misinterpretation of skaldic poetry or to magnify the brutality of the Viking world. (The Christian world loved to describe them as a sort of demonic wound.)

The Viking Calendar

The Vikings didn't have the four seasons that we have today. They had only two seasons, summer and winter, each one with six months. They didn't count the years as we do today but counted them after special events.

The Vikings counted the months from new moon to new moon or from full moon to full moon.

The moon was important to the Vikings for the tracking of time. However, the sun had a more central role not only because it brought light and life but also because, when the sun was high in the sky, it was possible to work the land growing crops.

The winter months were Gormánuður, Ýlir, Mörsugur, Þorri, Goa, and Einmánuður.

The summer months were Harpa, Skerpla, Sólmánuður, Heyannir, Tvímánuður, and Haustmánuður.

Gormánuður

The first winter month was called Slaughter month (October 14th –November 13th). On the first day, they held a feast, called Veturnettr or Haustblót, in honor of the God Freyr, thanking him for the harvest.

Ýlir

The second winter month was called Jol Month but is also known with the Yule name (November 14th –December 13th). Ýlir is also one of many Odin names. This was the time of year when Odin traveled around Midgard more than in the other months, visiting the locals. The children put hay inside socks as gifts for his horse Sleipnir, and Odin might give them a small gift in exchange. The Yule month was connected to fertility and linked to growing crops.

Mörsugur

The third winter month was called Bone Marrow Sucking month (December 14th – January 12th). This was the month of the Winter Solstice, which mostly falls on December 21st

Þorri

The fourth winter month was also called Thorri (January 13th – February 11th) and the Vikings held the feast of Torrablot. The night before the beginning of this month, a woman will walk outside her house and welcome Thorri inside, just as she would for any other guest. Possibly, Thorri was some kind of Norse mythical winter figure, the son of "Snow." In this month, the men could choose a day to be celebrated. However, if they choose a day with bad weather, it could be seen as a negative sign for them.

Goa

The fifth winter month (February 12th – March 13th) might have been dedicated to the daughter of Thorri and was known as Women's Month. This was the time when men focused on taking good care of their women.

Einmánuður

The sixth winter month was called "One Month" (March 14th – April 13th) and was dedicated to boys. March 21st is the Vernal Equinox and it was traditional to have a feast celebrating fertility.

Harpa

The first summer month was named Harpa (April 14th – May 13th). On the first day of this month, they held the summer blót, the third sacrificial feast, for the God Odin, to ensure victory in war and good luck on their travels. Harpa was the month dedicated to girls.

Skerpla

The second summer month was named Skerpla (May 14th – June 12th). This was a woman's name but it is unclear what the origin of the name is. The name "Skerpla" might refer to growth.

Sólmánuður

The third summer month was called the Sun Month (June 13th – July 12th). This was the month of the Summer Solstice, which mostly falls on June 21st.

Heyannir

The fourth summer month meant Hay Harvest (July 13th – August 14th). It was named "haymaking" and was the month of the drying and harvesting of hay.

Tvímánuður

The fifth summer month meant Two Month (August 15th – September 14th). This was the month when grain was harvested.

Haustmánuður

The last summer month meant Harvest Month (September 15th – October 13th). As we can see according to the months' names, the Vikings were mainly farmers and depended on the weather.

Days of the Week

Today, most of the days of the week are associated with the Nordic Gods.

Sunday

This day was dedicated to the sun and was also called Sunnudagr.

Monday

This day was dedicated to the moon and was also called Mánadagr.

Tuesday

This day was dedicated to the God Týr and was also called Týsdagr.

Wednesday

This day was dedicated to Odin and was also called Óðinsdagr.

Thursday

This day was dedicated to Thor and was also called Þórsdagr.

Friday

This day was dedicated to Frigg or Freyja and was also called Frjádagr.

Saturday

This day was dedicated to bathing and was also called Laugardagr.

Viking Ships

The Viking ships represented one of the greatest expressions of Northern European naval technology between the ninth and thirteenth centuries. Built to be fast, light, and resistant, they possessed characteristics that made them suitable for both the open sea and navigation in the shallow waters of coasts and rivers.

Norse peoples used mainly two types of ships: warships and goods transport vessels. The former were long, light, and fast, while the latter were made by focusing attention on strength and load capacity.

The boats used for war expeditions were not real warships in the modern sense of the term but, rather, ships for the transport of troops. Not having heavy weapons or rostrums that could damage the enemy ships, they often became real floating platforms that allowed the Norse infantry to attack the enemy melee.

The Viking ships used in the war were characterized by a long, thin, and light hull, with a draft often less than a meter that allowed them to not only overcome a shallow and treacherous bottom but also land on any beach simply by dragging the boat ashore. The ratio between length and width was generally 7 to 1.

One of the characteristics of many Viking ships (with the exception of those used for transporting goods or for long journeys by sea) was the symmetrical structure: Stern and bow were almost identical and made it possible to maneuver the boat in an agile and fast way, performing fast course changes without having to engage in circular maneuvers.

This feature was very useful when navigating between icebergs and sea ice—a situation in which quick and sudden changes of direction are required.

Warships had two methods of propulsion: sailing and oars. In the open sea, the sails made it possible to travel much faster than did the oars and to cover long distances without unnecessarily tiring the crew.

The sails could be hoisted or lowered very quickly. According to some tests carried out on modern reproductions of Norse boats, in just 90 seconds it was possible to install the mast and deploy the sail.

The ships were not equipped with rowing benches. To save space, the crew sat on crates containing their personal belongings. The crates were of a size that allowed a rower to sit at the right height to maneuver his oar.

The structure of the hull of a warship allowed it to reach incredible speeds for a boat of the time. The average navigation was around 9-18 km/h but, under favorable conditions, a Viking ship could reach a maximum speed of almost 30 km/h.

Viking ships can be classified according to the hull characteristics or construction details. However, the most common classification is based on the number of rowing stations.

Karvi

The karvi boat was the smallest of the Viking ships. To be suitable for military use, it had to have at least thirteen seats for rowers, even if any boat with six or more seats (up to sixteen) was generally classified as karvi.

These ships had a length/width ratio of 4: 5: 1 and were "multifunctional" ships, used for trade as well as for transporting troops to war. The evolution of karvi ships, the knarr, allowed for long ocean journeys during the Viking expansion era.

Knarr

Knarr-type ships were used for long journeys at sea and for transporting goods. They had a wider, deeper, and shorter hull than did battleships (with a length/width ratio very similar to that of the karts), which made these boats capacious and maneuverable by a small crew.

The knarr were generally 16 meters long and five meters wide and could carry up to 24 tons of cargo. Using the knarr, Norse peoples explored the whole of the Mediterranean, exchanged goods along the Baltic, and transported supplies to the most distant colonies of the Atlantic, such as Iceland and Greenland.

Snekkja

The snekkja was a thin military ship with at least 20 seats for rowers and capable of carrying 41 men. It was generally 17 meters long, 2-3 meters wide, and equipped with a draft of only half a meter.

The snekkja was the most common military vessel. The Norwegians built them with a deeper draft than did the Danes, to be able to easily cross the fjords and overcome the Atlantic climate without too many problems.

These ships did not need ports to dock. They were simply transported to the shore or beached. Their low weight also allowed an "arm" transport to overcome small stretches of land.

Skeid

These were warships larger than the snekkja and equipped with at least 30 seats for rowers. A skeid could carry 70-80 men and could exceed 30 meters in length. Roskilde 6, a Viking skeid discovered in 1996 and dating back to the year 1052, was 37 meters long.

Drakkar

The information we have about the Viking drakkar comes mainly from historical sources and sagas. Apparently, the only difference between a skeid and a drakkar was the type of hull decoration. The drakkar had carved bows, shaped like menacing beasts such as snakes or dragons.

According to one of the interpretations provided by archeology, these decorations served to keep at bay the sea monsters that, according to Norse mythology, populated the sea

Some of the most famous ships found are:

Nydam's Ship

An oak-wood ship discovered in the Nydam bog and dating from the years 310-320 AD. The ship is 23 meters long and 4 meters wide; it could hold up to 15 couples of rowers and weighed about three tons.

The Drakkar of Oseberg

Not really a drakkar but a karvi, it is 21 meters long and 5 meters wide, with a tree 10 meters high. It is estimated that the sail had a surface of 90 square meters and allowed the boat to reach a speed of 10 knots. The ship was used for the burial of two women whose identities remain a mystery.

Gokstad Ship

A ninth-century boat discovered in Gokstad, Norway. It is currently the largest Norwegian Viking ship ever brought to light. The boat is 23.80 meters long and 5 meters wide and was probably able to accommodate 32 rowers and a 110-square-meter sail, capable of pushing the ship at a speed of about 12 nodes.

Roskilde 6

The largest Viking ship ever discovered, at 36 meters long. It was discovered in Roskilde, Denmark. In 1070, the ship was deliberately sunk, along with four other boats, to block sea access to the city of Roskilde.

Berserker

The Berserkers were terrible pagan warriors sacred to Odin, dressed in bear or wolf skins. Boldness, bravery, and strength: These were some of the typical virtues of the warriors and heroes of the ancient Norse sagas. Being a Viking meant facing the stormy sea, plundering, killing, and raping without mercy, because the strongest always triumphs over the weakest.

Viking society was totally imbued with violence. Even today, when we approach the ancient Norse, we read of battles, bloody feuds, and duels to the death. Not for this reason, we must think that it was an anarchist society without rules. However, the violence itself was the pillar of the law and served to stem the uncontrolled outbreak of the same.

While it may seem unlikely, the warriors of the north followed a strict code of laws and rules that often also referred to honor. The battles, however bloody and brutal, were the place where they could be put on show and become famous, and they were regulated by unwritten codes.

But there is a category of warriors who went beyond any rule—men in full rule, who were closer to the world of Gods and beasts. These were the Berserkers, the fearsome bear or wolf warriors of sagas and legends. The etymology of the name, although discussed, seems to come from the Norwegian words "berr," which means bear, and "sarkr," which means knit, to create a meaning of "bear ties" or "bear garments."

The berserkers were sacred men. Their entire lives were dedicated to Odin. At the dawn of Viking society, they lived in small communities, usually in the thick of the forest or in uninhabited areas, where they hunted and performed rituals in the name of Odin and the Gods.

With the start of the Viking invasions in England and throughout Europe, the bear warriors began to sail with the raiders, thus exporting their fame throughout Europe. In battle, everyone feared the berserkers. Often, they did not wear armor, only bear or wolf furs. (Those who wore wolf skins were called ulfheðnar, "wolf heads"). Armed with swords and axes, they unleashed their fury without following any rule. They charged the enemy with their heads out of the wall of shields and raged against the bodies of the fallen.

Their wild way of fighting was often due to the use of hallucinogenic substances or drugs that led them to full madness. The stage of complete self-alteration was called Berserkesgrang (becoming Berserker) and was achieved through the use of hallucinogenic and poisonous mushrooms (such as amanita muscaria) or through the intake of very large quantities of alcohol.

This brought them to such ecstasy and fury that, in battle, they did not feel the wounds and sometimes even attacked their own companions. The mere presence of a Berserker could have caused so much terror in the enemy that he would run away. Their performances were so renowned that more than one Scandinavian king hired them as bodyguards. The long use of drugs and the complete immersion in such a violent world often led them to alterations of character and real mental illnesses such as hysteria, epilepsy, and outbursts of uncontrolled fury.

Before a battle, they bit their own shields out of excitement and howled and growled like wild beasts. Their fame was, therefore, not the most flattering: assassins, looters, and rapists. The Berserkers were so feared but also removed from society because they did not follow any order or law. Their only law was violence.

With the triumph of Christianity, Odin's crazy warriors (being proudly pagan) were seen less and less positively until they finally disappeared with the deities they had worshiped. They remained alive in the legends and in the poems, imperishable manifestos of their deeds.

CHAPTER 2: THE ORIGIN OF KNOWLEDGE

The Volva's Prophecy

The Prophecy of the Valley, which in a few stanzas evokes that Nordic wisdom from the creation of the world to its destruction, is one of the most beautiful reviews of the Norse myths.

The volva sat outside her home when Odin came before her and stared at her without speaking.

"What do you want to know? Why do you test me?" the volva snapped. "I know everything, Odin! I know where Heimdallr hid his horn, under the sacred tree that rises in the sky. And I know about that roar of clayey waters at its roots, where you paid your pledge. I know where you hid the eye, Odin! In the famous Mímisbrunnr spring! And you, do you know maybe more? "

Odin recognized the prophetic gift of the volva and gave her rings and necklaces. He gave her wise advice and gave her the rod of prophecy. Her eyes saw beyond the confines of the world, into the deeper past and the more remote future. There was no creature in the Nine Worlds that could push his gaze further than she.

She stood up and asked for silence. Then she began to prophesy.

"You want, Odin, that I fully narrate the ancient stories of the world, the ones I remember before the others. Well, I remember the giants, born in the beginning, who generated me and raised me. I remember nine worlds, and a huge tree whose nine roots penetrate and support them. When time was beginning, only Ymir lived. There was no sand and there was no sea, there were no cold waves. No land could be distinguished nor was there a sky above it. The abysses opened wide and no grass grew anywhere. Until, one day, the sons of Borr raised the lands, they who created the vast Midgard. The sun shone from the south on the rocky bottoms and then the ground was filled with green shoots.

"The sun, companion to the moon, stretched out his right hand towards the edge of the sky. The sun did not know where his court was, the stars did not know their home, the moon was unaware of its power. Then the Gods went to the thrones of judgment, the holy deities, and deliberated in assembly.

"They gave a name to the night and to the lunar phases, in the morning and at noon, and in the afternoon and in the evening, and so began to count the years.

"The Æsir gathered in the camp of Iðavǫllr, and here they raised altars and temples, lit fires, and forged tongs and other utensils, and created so many riches that there was never a golden shortage between them. Rich and happy, they played chess in that court, until three young girls, daughters of powerful giants beyond imagination, came from Jotunheim.

"Then the Gods went to the thrones of judgment, the holy deities, and in the assembly, they deliberated. It was necessary to decide who should create the hosts of the dvergar from the blood of the bones of Ymir. Motsognir was the most excellent of all the dwarves and the second was Durinn. Many dvergar were taken from the earth and were given human figures. The list of dwarf ancestors will be remembered as long as men live.

"And then, finally, three Æsir returned home, when they found Askr and Embla on the ground, the ash and the elm, without strength and without destiny. They had no breath, no soul, no vital heat, no gestures and nor was their appearance kind. Odin gave them destiny, Hoenir gave them soul, and Lodurr gave them a kindly appearance and color.

"I know an ash tree rises, called Yggdrasill. It always rises green, from the sources of Urdarbrunnr, a high trunk lapped by clay waters. From its branches, the dew falls on the valleys. From those waters that stretch out under the tree come three girls of great wisdom. The first is named Urd, the other Verdandi. Skuld is the third. They engrave runes on the tables, decide life, and establish the fate of men.

"I remember the first clash there was in the world, when the Gods hit Gullveig with spears and set her on fire. They burned her three times. Three times she was reborn and was still alive! They had called her 'shining,' and she was a fortune-teller who was an expert in prophecy. He came into the houses and, with his magical rods, full of sinister power, enchanted the senses and duped the evil brides. Then the Gods went to the thrones of judgment, the holy deities, and deliberated in assembly.

"They discussed whether the Æsir had to pay a tax or whether they were entitled to compensation. Odin threw his spear and began the first war ever seen in the world. The Vanir broke the wooden palisades and invaded the city of Æsir. Then the Gods went to the thrones of judgment, the holy deities, and deliberated in assembly. They wondered who had put the evil on earth and who had given Freyja, Odr's bride, to the giants.

"Then Thor got up, filled with anger. He didn't wait a moment when he heard about these misdeeds. Solemn oaths were broken and the most sacred pacts they had sealed were broken.

"I see the Valkyrie coming from a far, long distance. Skuld holds the shield. The second is Skogul. Then there are Gunnr, Hildr, Gondul, and Geirskogul. These are the girls of Herjan, who ride through the earth, the Valkyrie.

"I see a bloody sacrifice for Baldr. I see the hidden destiny prepared for Odin's son. A twig of mistletoe grew straight on the fields, thin and beautiful. From that fragile wood, a painful and fatal spear was made. Höder threw it.

"Vali, born before time, was one night old when he started fighting. He neither washed his hands nor combed his head until he could drag his brother's killer to the stake. But Frigg wept in Fensalir the pain of the whole Valhalla. And you, do you know maybe more? I see lying in the woods below Hveralund a figure that resembles Loki. Sigyn sits there, beside his groom, not at all enthusiastic about him. And you, do you know maybe more?

"A stream of daggers and swords flows from the east, through icy valleys like poison. They call it Slidr. To the north, in the Nidavellir, is the golden court of the Sindri lineage; but another court is located in Okolnir. It is the beer hall of the giant Brimir. But I see a third room, hidden by the sun, in Nastrandir. It has north-facing doors. Drops of poison rain down through the roof hole. The roof is formed by the intertwined backs of snakes. I see men come to that place, having forded insidious torrents, perjury, murderers, and seducers. There, Nidhogg sucks the corpses and the wolves devour its flesh. And you, do you know maybe more?

"An old woman sits in the east, in the forest of Jarnividr, and there she raises wolves, a lineage of Fenrir. From those beasts, one will come in the form of a giant to destroy the sun. It feeds on the lives of men devoted to death, bloodstains the houses of the Gods. In the summers that will come, the light of the sun will become dark, times of betrayal await us. And you, do you know maybe more?

"He sits down there on the hill and plays the harp, the happy Egger, who guards the herds of the giantesses. He sings a rooster with red feathers next to him in the wood of the birds. His name is Fjalarr. But another rooster, Gullinkambi, sings with the Æsir, who re-awaken the heroes. And a third rooster, red like soot, sings underground, in the halls of Hel.

"Ferocious the hellhound Garmr barks before Gnipahellir: The laces will break and the wolf will run. I have much wisdom: I see from afar the terrible destiny that hangs over the Gods. Brothers will be hurt and they will kill each other, family relationships will be forgotten. Violence and perversion will fill the world. A time of axes and swords, the shields will shatter: a time of wind and wolves, the world will collapse. There will not be a man who will want to spare another.

"The giants, sons of Mimir, are agitated, while the powerful sound of the Gjallarhorn announces the fulfillment of destiny. It is Heimdallr to blow into the horn while Odin speaks with Mimir's head. The ancient Yggdrasill ash shakes and trembles when the giants free themselves. All are taken by terror, on the road to the underworld, because the fire of Surtr is about to swallow them. What looms over the Æsir? What looms over the elves? Jotunheim is shaking, the Gods are gathered in the assembly. The dwarves, lords of the rocks, stand before the stone doors and moan with terror. And you, do you know maybe more?

"Hrymr, the king of the giants, comes from the east, holding the shield before him. Furious, Jormungandr twists, a huge snake that shakes the waves. The eagle screeches and tears at the corpses. Sail Naglfar, the ship of the dead. But another ship sets sail from the east. It is the one that leads the giants of Muspelheim to the sea. Loki holds the helm. The army of monsters is advancing and the wolf is in the lead. From the south comes Surtr, cloaked in flames. The Gods stand in defense with swords lit by the sun. The rocks are breaking, the giantesses are collapsing, men are embarking on the last journey, the sky is crashing. And here, another pain comes to Frigg when Odin goes to fight with the wolf (and Freyr moves against Surtr). Thus, Frigg's spouse falls. But here comes Vidarr, son of Odin, to face the beast. With both hands, he thrusts his sword to his heart, and so he avenges his father. And here comes Thor to oppose Jormungandr. Furious, he hits Midgard's defender, then steps back nine steps and collapses. The sun becomes dark, the earth sinks into the waters, the stars disappear from the firmament. The steam hisses with fire and the flames rise to touch the sky. Ferocious the hellhound Garmr barks before Gnipahellir: The laces will break and the wolf will run. I have much wisdom: I see from afar the terrible destiny that hangs over the Gods.

"And, once again, I see the earth emerging from the sea, freshly green. The falls cascade down, the eagle flies high, she who hunts for fish from the mountains. The Æsir are found in Idavoll and talk about the mighty snake that was tight around the world; they remember the great deeds of past times and of Odin, who all knew the runes. And there they will find in the grass those wonderful gold chessboards that they had once possessed. Although not sown, the fields will produce crops. All evil will disappear and Baldr will return. Baldr and his brother Höder, happy warrior Gods, will inhabit the victorious ruins of Odin's ancient home. Do you know maybe more? I see a court covered in gold, rising, even more beautiful than the sun, high in the sky, at Gimlé. Groups of brave will live there and be happy forever.

"But at the end of everything, he will come to his kingdom who rules everything from above. And the dragon of darkness, Nidhogg, that shimmering serpent, will fly from the Nidafjoll Mountain, over the plain bearing the bodies of the dead under its wings."

This was the prophecy that the volva gave to men and the Gods: a harsh song, difficult, fast, and full of puzzles. Deep knowledge is necessary to interpret it.

But in a few pairs of semiverses, how much wisdom! The entire universe is enclosed there, from the abyssal abyss to the creation of the world, from destruction to rebirth. Space and time tightly intertwined with each other ... until the final judgment.

And in these loud and powerful verses, the volva had recalled the ancient golden age and how the war between Æsir and Vanir had put an end to it by bringing evil into the world. He had well warned that the destinies are all in the hands of the Nornirs, gathered around the Urdarbrunnr spring. He had untangled the threads of the drama of the world, which were tangled around the fatal episode of Baldr's murder, and, following them through time, had shown how these facts would lead the world to fall into the darkness of the last days. The volva had still pointed out giants and wolves, damned souls and snakes, the enemies that would have annihilated the universe in what would have been the day of Ragnarök. But he had opened a hope together, showing how the cyclical nature of time would one day bring the world back, beyond the purifying fire, into a restored happy age...

And as soon as he had said all these things, the volva sank into the earth.

Ymir and the Creation of the World

At the beginning of time, there was nothing we can see around us today. There was no earth or sky above, no sea bordered with beaches, no plants, no grass, or other living creatures. The primordial aspect of the universe, according to Norse beliefs, was represented by an enormous, boundless abyss, the Ginnungagap: a chaotic, obscure, formless nothingness, dominated by powerful and uncontrollable energies that stirred in a primordial chasm of the times. However, the fascinating and desolate emptiness that preceded the creation of the universe was not a lack of substance but, rather, a lack of discernible form.

North of the Ginnungagap lay the dark region of eternal ice, dominated by frost and fog, called Niflheim, the "house of fog." To the south, instead, there was the Muspellsheim, the land of fire, a region dominated by burning flames and unbearable heat where fire reigned supreme.

At the center of the Niflheim, there was the well of Hvergelmir, from which the eleven primordial rivers, called Élivágar, gushed with sound boiling and stirring at very high temperatures. These are their names: Svol, Gunnthra, Fjorm, Fimbulthul, Slidr, Hrid, Sylgr, Ylgr, Vid, Leiptr and Gjoll. These fell into the Ginnungagap, creating immense icy waves which, breaking down, covered the whole Ginnungagap with a dense icy foam.

The Élivágar came so far from their source that the surface poison that accompanied them hardened as a slag of combustion and became ice. Where this ice stopped, a drizzle fell which became frost and covered the whole Ginnungagap in layers. This is the scenario, dominated by the presence of two opposite but complementary poles, in which the events leading to the birth of the universe and the Norse Gods took place.

Indeed, from the icy Niflheim region and the inflamed region of Muspellsheim, lava and ice continually flowed and collided in the Ginnungagap void, forming particles of melted frost charged with life. From the fusion of these opposites, two creatures were born: Ymir the progenitor of the race of giants [jotnar], an androgynous giant who could cover the whole earth, animated by a very powerful fire, and the cow, Auðhumla, that fed him.

But the drops from which Ymir was born contained the particles of poison that had been splashed by the Élivágar. This was the reason why Ymir was, yes, wise but also evil and why all his descendants were evil.

Despite his size, Ymir was only a newborn whose main occupations were eating and sleeping. Because he was unable to go with females, his sons were born of him by spontaneous generation.

While he slept, he began to sweat profusely. The sweat from his left arm generated two giants, a male and a female, while the sweat of his legs generated Þrúðgelmir (Thrudhgelmir), a six-headed giant who later generated Belgermir.

Time passed and, while the giant child slept, the Adhumula cow drew the necessary nourishment for itself by licking the salt of the icy stones present in Niflheim. On the first day, towards evening, he brought to light a man's hair, the next day his head and the third day the whole person.

This form, androgynous like Ymir, was Buri, the first of the Gods. He was beautiful and strong but alone. So, he gave birth to a son named Bor, who then joined the giantess Bestla, daughter of Blalþorn, one of the giants generated by Ymir. They had three children. The first was called Odin, the second Vili, and the third Vé.

The sons of Borr—Odin, Vili, and Vé—engaged in a furious struggle with Ymir. They killed him with a violent blow to the head and dragged his body into the middle of the Ginnungagap.

Out of his carcass came worms, to which Odin and his brothers infused intelligence and conscience. The worms then became dwarves, creatures who went to live in the bowels of the Earth and who, thanks to their skills as artisans, produced the great treasures of the Gods.

And from that body, they drew the world, which they raised above the abyss. With the flesh of the ancient giant, they made the earth, and they raised the mountains with his bones. They made stones and boulders with his teeth, jaws, and bone splinters. The hair served to create the forests. They threw his brain into the air and so came the clouds.

They placed Ymir's immense skull above it and the sky was drawn from it. At the four corners, four dwarves were placed to support him: Austri, Vestri, Nordri, and Sudri. Their names indicated the four cardinal points.

With the blood gushing from the wounds of Ymir, in which all the giants had drowned, the sons of Borr made the ocean and tied it tightly to the earth, tying it around like a ring. It seems, to most men, impossible to cross.

Subsequently, the Earth was raised from the sea abysses and to its extremities, the three brothers created the territory destined then to the giants, the Jotunheim, in the extreme enclosure of the world.

The kingdom of men was created and then immediately protected and separated from the territory of the giants by a mighty fortification, created using Ymir's eyebrows, later called "Midgard," the middle kingdom.

In the blood of Ymir, the three sons of Borr drowned all the giants that had descended from him. The only two to save themselves were the giants called Bergelmir and his wife.

It is not clear how Bergelmir managed to save himself. Some say that Bergelmir had climbed along with his wife to the top of a mill and had thus managed to escape the flood of blood. Others say that they both fled on a boat, perhaps a rough, hollowed-out trunk.

Whatever happened, Bergelmir and his wife, they say, were saved from the massacre and repaired far away. The descendants of the frost giants, the jotnar, would descend from them.

After the creation of the world, Odin, Vili, and Vé took the sparks that flew in the air, sprayed out from Múspellsheimr, and placed them in the middle of the Ginnungahiminn, the sky of the abyss, above and below, to illuminate the sky and land.

At that time, the sun and the moon roamed free in the sky, completely unaware of their virtues and their destiny. The stars, likewise, had neither laws nor mansions. Thus, the sons of Odin put order in the firmament, giving all the stars a place and a role. Some they fixed in the vault of the sky, while for others they established a course to go. They took the course of the sun to the south and named it in the morning and in the evening, at noon and in the afternoon. They measured the phases of the moon and imposed on them an order and a duration. They set the mechanisms of the firmament, giving order and stability to the universe. The divisions of days and the calculation of months and years were established in this way. And so the computation of time began.

Time Elements and Other Cosmogonies

- The Day and the Night

A giant called Norfi lived in Jotunheim. He had a daughter whose name was Nótt (night), dark and brown like all the members of his lineage. She was given in marriage to a man named Naglfari. Their son was named Authr. Later, she was married to the one named Annarr and their daughter was Jord (land). Finally, he was married to Dellingr and their son was Dagr (day). He was as bright as his father.

The Gods wanted to celebrate so they took Nótt and Dagr, gave them two steeds, so fast that they could complete a full circle of the Earth in twelve hours, and two beautiful wagons, and placed them in the sky to run around the earth every day. First, he rode Nótt with the horse named Hrímfaxi, "hoarfrost mane." Every morning, the foam from its bite dripped on the earth, creating the dew rains in the valleys. Dagr's horse was called Skinfaxi, “shining mane.” Heaven and earth are illuminated by the splendor of his mane.

- The Sun and the Moon

A man called Mundilfari had two children. They were so beautiful and shining that he called his son Máni and his daughter Sól, like the moon and the sun, and gave this to the man named Glenr.

The Gods, however, could not bear that a common mortal, guided by pride, would take possession of the names of their creations, so they kidnapped both and placed them in the sky.

They placed Sól to guide the chariot that carries the sun, built by the Gods to illuminate the world with a spark taken in the Múspellheimr. The two horses were called Árvakr and Alsvithr. Under the shoulder blades of the steeds, the Gods placed two iron bellows to cool them during their run. Svalinn was the name of the shield that was placed before the sun. If it were taken from that place, the seas and mountains would flare up. Máni was responsible for the movements of the moon, as well as for the growth and decline of its phases.

And there was still a reason why Sól and Máni ran in the sky without ever stopping, and it was that they were eternally chased by two wolves...

Every day, the impressive chariot driven by the beautiful Sól moved from east to west and was chased by the wolf Skoll, the “traitor,” while Máni was chased by the wolf “Hati” (“hate” or “enemy”). Every month, it was said, Hati managed to bite the moon by removing a piece but each time the moon was able to move away and grow again.

– The Helper of the Moon

Two boys were called Bil and Hjúki and were the sons of Vithfinnr. One evening, they were moving away from Byrgir's well, carrying on their shoulders the stick called Símul and the bucket called Saeg. Máni kidnapped them from the earth to help regulate the phases of the moon.

These two children can be seen on the lunar disk, together with their stick and their bucket.

- The Lineage of the Wolves

An old female orc lived east of Midgard, in the iron tree forest, in Jarnividr. The old woman created giants in the form of wolves and raised them.

It was from this place that Skoll and Hati, sons of Hróthvitnir (Fenrir), came.

And it was also said that from this lineage came a very powerful wolf called Mánagarmr, "dog of the moon." He fed on the flesh of all the men who died and it would be him who, at the end of the world, would swallow the moon and smear the earth and sky with blood.

- Summer and Winter

What is the difference between hot summers and cold winters? Everyone knows how to explain it. Svásuthr was called the giant father of Sumar, "summer." He lived a life so happy that, from him, whatever was pleasant took its name. The father of Vetr, "winter," instead, was a giant who some say was called Vindsvalr; he was the son of Vásathr. They were strict relatives and cold-tempered, and Vetr had their character.

- The Sea, the Fire, and the Wind

The giants, who were very wise because their lineage went back to the origins of the world, had power over the elements of nature. It was said that an ancient giant called Fornjótr reigned over the icy lands of Finnland. From him descended a powerful and famous progeny: his sons, Aegir, Logi, and Kári.

Aegir was the lord of the sea. His bride was named Rán. She had a net with which she gathered the drowned and transported them to her home. The nine daughters of Hlér and Rán were the waves of the sea. They prepared the beer for which Irgir was rightly famous—so much so that it was in his room where the Gods gathered to drink and toast.

Logi was the devouring fire lord. He was called Hálogi, "exalted flame," and he was the ruler of the province that took his name, the Hálogaland.

Kári was the wind. His son Frosti, "cold" (also called Jǫkull), had power over cold and ice. The son of these was called Snær "snow". Snær also had three sons: Þorri "month of the fourth wind", the lord of the second half of winter, Fǫnn "sleet", and Mjǫll "fresh snow"; and a daughter, Drífa, "snow-storm."

Others, however, say that Logi and his sister Skjálf were the children of Frosti and that they avenged their father when he was killed by King Agni of the Ynglingar.

- Hraesvelgr, the Eagle of the Winds

Where does the wind come from? It is so strong that it shakes the vast seas and stirs the fire. However, strong as it is, it cannot be seen because it was done admirably.

In the northern part of the sky lived a giant called Hræsvelgr who looked like an eagle. When the wings moved, all the winds that blew on the world were formed beneath them.

Dvergar, from the Earth, the Straight of the Dwarves

The lineage of the dvergar, or dwarves, was formed underground, where they took life as worms in the dead flesh of Ymir, in his blood transformed into water and among his bones turned into stone. Thus, they were created from Brimir's blood and Bláinn's bones.

The Dvergar took up residence in the soft earth and mud, among the rocks and stones. Motsognir was the most famous among them. Another was named Durinn. He was created to bring back the secrets of the dwarven kingdom.

The names of many dvergar are remembered. First, the tradition includes Nordri, Sudri, Austri, and Vestri, the four dwarves who supported the sky at the cardinal points. And then Nýi and Níði, the two dvergar who ruled the full moon and the new moon.

An Ash and an Elm: Creation of Men by the Children of Borr

After creating the world and giving birth to the lineage of dwarves, the sons of Borr resumed their way home. Once on the shores of the sea, they found two trees tossed by the waves. They were an ash and an elm. Odin gave them their breath and life, Vili gave them reason and movement, and Vé gave them form, word, hearing, and sight. From those two inanimate trunks came the first human pair. The sons of Borr gave them names. The man was called Askr "ash tree" and the woman Embla "elm". The Gods gave them clothes, as Odin recalls:

"My clothes I gave in the fields to two wooden men. Great men believed themselves as they had clothes:

Naked, everyone is broken."

From this first couple came all humanity, to which was given a home in Midgard. This, at least, is what was told to King Gylfi during his journey to Asgard

An Ash and an Elm: Creation of Men by Odin, Hønir, and Lodurr

The volva attributed the creation of the first pair to Odin, Hønir, and Lodurr. They were returning to their home when they found Askr and Embla—the ash and the elm—on the ground, without strength and without a destiny. Odin breathed them, Hønir conceded his soul, and Lodurr gave them vitality and color.

What matters, in any case, is that a man and a woman rose from that ash tree and from that elm, by the will of the Gods. Askr and Embla were the progenitors of all humanity. To them and to their descendants, the Gods gave residence in Midgard.

The Nine Worlds

From the convulsive vicissitudes of creation, culminating in the sacrifice of Ymir, a new universal order had arisen, above the abyssal depths of the Ginnungahiminn, established and regulated by the Æsir. From the dismembered body of Ymir, an entire universe had arisen whose heavenly vault had been carved from the skull of the ancient giant. The sun and the moon, Sól and Máni, gave him light and warmth, marking the counting of time. Surrounding the universe was an outer ocean (úthaf) born of the deluge of blood that had ended the race of primordial giants.

The center of the universe was the Midgard, the "inner enclosure," where men dwelt, the children of Askr and Embla. The Gods had built around it a bastion created with Ymir's eyelashes, so as to protect the world of men from the jotnar, the frost giants, descendants of Bergelmir. These lived in

Utgard, the "outer enclosure," on the edge of the world, on the shores of the cosmic ocean.

The Gods, the álfars, the dvergar, and all the creatures dwelt in other worlds, in the deepest underground abysses or in inaccessible regions of the sky. There were many worlds, which the most learned said to be nine in number. The Élivágar, the cosmic rivers that flowed from the Hvergelmir spring, flowed through all these worlds, linking them in an uninterrupted and constant flow.

Life and support of the universe came from the great ash tree, Yggdrasill, whose trunk was the axis that connected earth, sky, and abysses, whose branches covered the firmament and whose three roots reached, respectively, the world of the Gods, that of the giants, and that of the dead.

"Nine worlds of remembrance," the volva had stated at the beginning of her prophetic song. These realms were nestled in the tree of life, Yggdrasil, held by his branches and roots, and were the homelands of various types of beings (the Gods, Goddesses, giants, humans, and more). All nine worlds would be destroyed at the end of the day during Ragnarök.

The first of the nine worlds was Midgard, the "middle fence," located at the center of the universe; the sons of men dwelled there. It was located in the middle of the world, just below Asgard. Midgard and Asgard were connected by the rainbow bridge Bifrǫst. Midgard was surrounded by an impassable ocean occupied by Jormungandr, the huge sea serpent. This serpent encircled the world entirely and bit his own tail.

The second world was Ásaheimr, from which came the Æsir. There was the city of Asgard, with its temples and buildings. The king was Odin. It was believed to have been placed in the sky. Odin, sitting in his throne Hliðskjálf, could observe everything that happened in all nine words. Into the gates of Asgard, there was Valhalla—the place where half of the souls of the Vikings that had a glorious death in battle found themselves in the afterlife. Asgard was the location of Urdarbrunnr, the well of Destiny.

The third world was Vanaheimr, the land of the Vanir, the masters of sorcery and magic lives. They were also known for their ability to predict the future. Though there is no precise data, it appears to have been west of Ásaheimr.

The fourth world was Jotunheim, the kingdom of the jotnar. It was located in the snowy regions on the outermost shores of the ocean at the ends of the world, in Utgard. Is was a place that consisted mostly of rocks, wilderness, and dense forests, and it was the home of the sworn enemies of the Æsir, the giants. One of the three wells, Mimir's well of wisdom, was located in the Jotunheim root of the ash tree Yggdrasil.

The fifth world was Álfheimr. The light elves, Ljósálfar, lived there. It seemed to be not far from the Ásaheimr. These beautiful creatures, considered the "guardian angels," were minor Gods of nature and fertility and helped humans with their knowledge of magical powers. They also often inspired art, music, and other sorts of creativity.

The sixth world was the Svartálfaheimr, which lay underground. The Dvergar and Døkkálfar lived there and were ruled by Hreidmar. These masters of craftsmanship lived under the rocks, in caves and underground. They crafted for the Gods of Asgard many powerful gifts like Gungnir, Odin's spear, as well as the magical golden ring Draupnir.

The seventh world was Niflheim, the coldest and darkest region, the homeland of mist, primordial darkness, and ice. It was located in the north, although it sometimes appeared to be situated in the abyss. It was one of the oldest worlds and was originally part of the Ginnungagap.

The eighth world was the fiery Múspellsheimr, which was also part of the Ginnungagap in the beginning. This was a burning hot place filled with lava, fire, flames, sparks, and soot. It was unbearable to foreigners who did not have their origin there. Múspellsheimr was ruled by the giant Surtr and was the home of the fire giants. Surtr was Æsir's sworn enemy, and when Ragnarök, "the end of the world," came, Surtr would ride out with his flaming sword in his hand and attack Asgard, "the home of the Gods," turning it into a blazing inferno.

The ninth and last world was the kingdom of Hel. It was a very grim and cold place. Any Viking who entered it would never feel joy and happiness. It was ruled by Hel, the daughter of Loki, and was the place of all the thieves, the murderers, and the Vikings who had died dishonorable deaths and were not brave enough to go to Valhalla and feast with the Gods.

It was found in the deepest and darkest area of the universe, characterized by frost, rain, humidity, and fog. Below was Niflhel, the "misty hell." The souls of the wicked, after having passed through Hel, seemed to go to that place.

Except for Midgard, all of them were invisible worlds that could be manifested in some aspect of the visible world (Jotunheim with physical wilderness, Hel with the grave, and Asgard with the sky).

Having created the universe, the Æsir went to a remote place in the center of the world and, on the top of inaccessible mountains, built a fortress called Asgard.

In Asgard, the Gods built their homes, as well as many buildings and magnificent temples. In this place, they went to live with their families. As soon as Asgard's building was finished, Odin appointed twelve Gods who, along with him, would be the rulers of the fortress. This happened in a place at the center of the citadel, called Íðavǫllr, the "vortex field," which, judging by the name, seems to confirm what is said: That is, Asgard is at the perfect center of the world, near the axis around which the skies rotate. All decisions regarding destiny and world government came from that place.

We do not know where Asgard arose. It is said that King Gylfi arrived there after a long journey and that he learned the secrets of ancient things there. However, in what lands he directed his steps and which mountains he crossed is information that has not been handed down. Some historians, playing on an easy etymology, argue that Asgard was in Asíá, east of the river Tanais (the Don), in a land called Ásaheimr or Ásaland. These historians say that from that place, the Æsir would move and eventually reach the countries in the north of the earth (by some called Evrópá and by others Eneá), where they would have established kingdoms and founded the royal dynasties of Danmǫrk, Nóregr, and Svíþjóð. However, this is an explanation that does not convince the most shrewd mythographers.

Others say that the city of Asgard, with its wonderful palaces, was in the sky and was connected to the earth by the Bifrǫst, the rainbow bridge. In fact, we know that there were many skies. Above ours, towards the south, there was a second heaven called Andlangr. Above this, there was a third heaven called Víðbláinn, which was the supreme one. In the part of this sky that turned to the south was the wonderful Gimlé room. On the day of Ragnarök, when heaven and earth would be wiped out, Gimlé would resist the destructive fire and welcome good and righteous men. But whoever lived in those very high and remote places, even the Gods did not know. They believed that only the Ljósarfars lived there.

If Asgard rose in the center of the world, the borders of the universe were defined by the outer ocean (úthaf). This place, placed outside the bastion raised to protect the "middle enclosure" of Midgard, was called Utgard, "outer enclosure." Here lived the frost giants, whose ruler was Hrímr. The King of Utgard was Útgarðaloki.

In the outer ocean, Odin threw the serpent Jormungandr. But this, coming into contact with the vivifying waters of the úthaf, grew out of all proportion until its coils surrounded the whole world and, turning on itself, bit its tail. In this way, Jormungandr marked the boundary between the world and the cosmic abyss, being itself the extreme limit of the universe. It was also called Miðgarðsormr, "serpent of Midgard."

When on the day of Ragnarök, Jormungandr would rise to fall upon the world, the waves of the úthaf would break their limits and fall on the earth, flooding and exterminating mankind. Then the serpent would spit out so much poison that all the sky and the earth would be sprayed.

Yggdrasil, the Tree of Life

The nine worlds are supported by the Yggdrasill ash, a high trunk lapped by clear waters. Yggdrasill is the most impressive and the best of trees, the evergreen symbol of good and evil and of the eternal flow of life, a powerful plant metaphor that unites heaven and earth in an inescapable destiny. Its branches spread over the whole world and cover the sky. From them, drops of honey fall on the earth, like drops of dew, from which the bees feed. Three roots support the tree and branch out in three different directions.

The first root is lowered into the deepest depths; some say it arrives in Helheimr, the kingdom of the dead, while others say that it extends instead into Niflheim, from which it would eventually reach the source of Hvergelmir. Below this root is the serpent Nidhogg. With him, there are so many snakes that no language can count them.

The second root goes, instead, towards Jotunheim, the land where the giants live, and arrives at the source of Mímisbrunnr. Here, knowledge and knowledge are hidden and the one who owns the well is called Mimir. He is full of wisdom because he draws from the source with the Gjallarhorn horn. Access to the source, however, is prohibited by his wise guardian, God Mimir. He allowed Odin to drink at the source of wisdom but for a high price: The father of the Gods had to sacrifice his eye, left as a pledge.

The third root goes towards the Ásaheimr and reaches the sacred source of Urdarbrunnr, in the place where the Æsir hold counsel every day. Under the ash tree, in front of that source, there is a magnificent dwelling and in it live the Nornir Urd, Verdandi, and Skulld. They are the ones who water Yggdrasil with miraculous spring water to keep it alive. Yggdrasil would dry and rot if the Nornirs did not pour water from the Urdarbrunnr spring onto the tree trunk and branches every day.

In that source, moreover, live two swans. From them came the whole race of these birds.

On the top, there is a gigantic eagle, custodian of ancient secrets, whose beating of wings originates the winds that sweep the world of men. The eagle constantly monitors the horizon to warn the Gods of the arrival of their enemies.

Under the root of the ash tree that stretches out into the Niflheimr, horrible snakes are found, more than any fools imagine: Góinn and Móinn (sons of Grafvitnir), Grábakr and Grafvǫlluðr, Ófnir and Sváfnir. But the most fear-some is Nidhogg, in constant combat with the eagle. All these monsters incessantly gnaw at the root of the ash. The messenger of the skirmishes between the two animals is the squirrel Ratatoskr, who runs up and down the trunk of the ash tree, reporting the insults exchanged between them. The struggle between the eagle and the snake represents the eternal battle between light and darkness, wisdom and ignorance.

Four deer leap between the branches of the ash tree and bite its sharp leaves. They are called Dáinn, Dvalinn, Duneyrr, and Duraþrór.

Because of all these creatures that live between the roots and the branches of the ash tree (the snakes, the four deer, the squirrel, and the two birds of prey), Yggdrasill would dry and rot if the Nornir who live near Urdarbrunnr did not draw from the water source every day and pour that clay on the ash tree and spread it on the tree trunk and branches.

In addition to the Yggdrasill ash tree, scholars know the names of two other important trees. one is called Léraðr and the other Mímameiðr.

The Eikþyrnir deer and the Heiðrún goat feed on the leaves of Læraðr (or Léraðr). The deer is found in Valhalla. Drops fall from its horns, so large that they form, in the depths of the world, the well of Hvergelmir, from which all the rivers that flow through the universe originate. On the other hand, the goat is on the roof of Valhalla and from there it easily grazes on the leaves of the tree. From its breasts flows the mead on which the einherjar feed.

On the tree Mímameiðr, the rooster Víðófnir, enemy of the giants, waits to announce the day of Ragnarök.

However, many think that the Læraðr and the Mímameiðr are nothing other than different names for the same Yggdrasill ash.

Bifrost, the Rainbow Bridge

It is the ásbrú, the rainbow bridge, which provides a passage from earth to heaven. This bridge is named Bifrǫst, and it was the Gods themselves who built it, with art and profound wisdom. A difficult passage, the rainbow bridge is accessible only to those who know how to access it.

Bifrǫst has three colors, a perfect manifestation of sacredness, and red as the fire that burns.

The other end of the bridge, on which runes are engraved, reaches the foot of the Himinbjǫrg fortress, where Asgard's gates open wide. In that place, Heimdallr, the sentinel of the Gods, watches day and night, ensuring that the giants do not have access to the rainbow bridge and do not attempt to climb the sky.

Though fragile in appearance, the Bifrǫst bridge is solid and made with art. It will last as long as the world lasts. However, it will collapse when Ragnarök comes. This is not surprising because then nothing in the universe will be spared.

The Gods ride every day along the Bifrǫst bridge when they go to the þing near the source of Urdarbrunnr. It is in that silent place, in the shadow of the great ash tree Yggdrasill, that they hold their assemblies. Only to Thor is transit on the bridge prohibited, as all of Bifrǫst would go up in flames under the wheels of his chariot. Therefore, he is forced to proceed on foot, fording a series of rivers: the Kǫrmt, the Ǫrmt, and the two Kerlaugar.

Hvergelmir and the Ancient Rivers

In Niflheim, the world of frost and fog, is the source of Hvergelmir, the primordial cauldron from which all the waters begin their journey. From the beginning of time, the eleven ancient rivers called Élivágar, whose glaciers melted in the heat of the Múspellheimr, gave rise to the giant Ymir. These are their names: Svǫl, Gunnþrá, Fjǫrm, Fimbulþul, Slidr, Hríð, Sylgr, Ylgr, Víð, Leiptr, and Gjǫll. Even today, from Hvergelmir, all the rivers that flow in the sky, in the earth, and in the underworld flow.

They say that Hvergelmir is fed by the drops flowing down the horns of the deer Eikþyrnir, which is found in Valhalla and feeds on the leaves of the Léraðr tree. From the same source comes one of the three roots of the Yggdrasill ash, and from below it is pinked by Nidhogg and other snakes.

Some rivers come out of the boiler of Hvergelmir and reach the sky, where they roar loudly around the abodes of the Gods. These are their names: Síð and Víð, Sekin and Ekin, Svǫl and Gunnþrá, Fjǫrm and Fimbulþul, Rin and Rennandi, Gipul and Gǫpul, and Gǫmul and Geirvimul. The rivers Þyn and Vin, Il and Hǫll, and Gráð and Gunnþráin are probably added to this. The Þund river also flows around Valhalla.

Other rivers descend into the world of men and, from there, pour down to the world of the dead. These are their names: Vína, Vegsvinn and Þjóðnuma, Nýt and Nǫt, Nǫnn and Hrǫnn, Slidr and Hríð, Sylgr and Ylgr, Víð and Ván, Vǫnd and Strǫnd, and Leiptr and Gjǫll.

Something can be added about the latter: The Slidr arrives from the east, crossing valleys of poison, and in its waters flow blades of swords and daggers. The Ván is born from the burr of the wolf Fenrir, which lies chained with its jaws held wide open by the blade of a sword. Finally, the river Gjǫll flows to the gates of Helheim; it crosses over the Gjallarbrú bridge, covered with gold, to which the maiden Móðguðr stands guard. On this bridge, Hermóðr galloped when he came to ask Hel to return Baldr.

Among infernal rivers, there remains Vaðgelmir, which must be waded by the men who lie or fight each other.

Finally, it is necessary to remember, in the computation of the rivers, the Kǫrmt, the Ǫrmt, and the two Kerlaugar, which Thor is forced to wade on foot every day when he goes to the assembly with the Gods, as the Bifrǫst bridge would go up in flames under the wheels of his wagon.

Speaking of cosmic rivers, we must not forget Ífing, which divides the earth of the Gods from that where the children of the giants dwell. As Odin explained to the wise Vafþrúðnir, the waters of this river will flow free until the end of time without ever freezing. They mark an impassable border that keeps the forces of destruction eternally far away.

It is, therefore, probable that the Ífing river is the same úthaf, the sea that surrounds the world. That even the ocean waters came from the Hvergelmir spring seems to be indicated by the fact that, according to what they say, the giant Hymir dwelt on the edge of the sky, "east of the Élivágar." However, what stretched not far from Hymir's house was, in fact, the úthaf, the outer sea, on which Thor sailed to catch the snake Jormungandr.

CHAPTER 3: NORSE GODS AND GODDESSES

Æsir and Vanir

The Æsir lived in a land called Ásaheimr at the center of the world. In this distant land, on the top of mountains so high that they almost touched the sky, the Gods raised the fortress of Asgard, where, among splendid buildings and magnificent temples, they went to live with their families and their children. From that high and remote place, the Æsir established their dominion over the world and their rule over the elements and the destiny of all beings.

But while the Æsir settled in their heavenly fortresses, another lineage chose to live in contact with the eternal cycles of the earth. Not much can be said of the Vanir. We do not know who they came from or who their rulers were. They lived in a remote land called Vanaheimr, whose location is uncertain, although some say it was west of Ásaheimr. Supernatural, mysterious, and powerful people, the Vanir were experts in magical practices, of which women, above all, were the depositories. Because of this science, they were able to see the future. The Vanir family was a society closed in on itself, jealous of its characteristics and peculiarities. Common was the practice of incest among them and it was not uncommon for sibling marriages to be celebrated.

In the past, says the volva, there was a war between the Æsir and the Vanir, a war that ended with a reconciliation between the two divine lineages. Hostages were exchanged, so some of the Æsir went to live in Vanaheimr, while some of the powerful Vanir were welcomed in Asgard.

Fourteen are the Gods [Æsir] of divine lineage who rule the city of Asgard, and, likewise, fourteen are the Goddesses [ásinjur], no less holy and powerful.

Lord of Asgard is Odin, and these are those who govern the fortress: Thor, Baldr, Njǫrðr, Freyr, Týr, Bragi, Heimdallr, Höder, Vidarr, Váli, Ullr, and Forseti, to which, fourteenth, must be added Loki.

These are the Goddesses: Frigg, Sága, Eir, Gefjun, Fulla, Freyja, Sjǫfn, Lofn, Vár, Vǫr, Syn, Hlín, Snotra, and Gná. Sól and Bil are also counted among the Goddesses, and we have already talked about them.

Odin, the principal and eldest of the Æsir, is called Allfǫðr, "father of all," because it is from him that all the Gods descend. Odin governs all things in the world and, although the other Gods are also powerful, they serve him, as children do with their father. Frigg is his bride.

Many are the sons of Odin. The first is Thor, whom Odin generated by joining with his own daughter, Jǫrð. Full of strength, Thor surpasses all living creatures. The bride of Thor is Sif, with the golden braids, with whom he had a son, Móði, and a daughter, Þrúðr. Another son, Magni, Thor generated with the giantess Járnsaxa. Ullr, a great archer and skier, is the son of Sif's first husband and, therefore, is a stepson of Thor.

Odin's second son, from Frigg, is Baldr. He is the best of the Æsir, handsome, wise, and kind. Everyone loves and respects him. His wife is Nanna, daughter of Nepr. Their son is Forseti, judge of the Gods. Baldr's brothers are the God Höder, who is blind, and the fast Hermóðr.

Odin is the father of many other Gods. The giantess Gríðr gave birth to Vidarr the silent, the strongest of the Æsir after Thor. Princess Rindr made him the father of the brave Váli. The brave Týr is also the son of Odin, although others say he is, rather, the son of the giant Hymir.

Among the other Gods, we count Bragi, supreme in eloquence and skilled in poetry and in the skaldic arts. His wife is Iðunn, the one who guards the apples that the Gods must eat when they grow old to become young again. And, again, we remember Heimdallr, Asgard's sentinel, who was raised at the beginning of time by nine mothers, all sisters. Finally, we must enumerate Loki, the deceiver's blacksmith, son of Fárbauti and Laufey. His work will be sadly known among the Gods and among men for as long as the world lasts.

A few we can add on the other divine lineage, that of the Vanir. We do not know their origin, nor do we know who their rulers were. Of the Vanir we know just the names of those who, after the war that opposed the two divine lineages, abandoned the Vanaheimr and moved into Asgard as hostages, sharing with the Æsir the abode and the divine rank.

These were Njǫrðr and his sons Freyr and Freyja. These two youth, according to the Vanir custom, Njǫrðr had from his own sister. With the Æsir, however, a union of such close relatives was not permitted.

Once in Asgard, Njǫrðr and his sons married in turn. The proud Skaði, daughter of the giant Þjazi, became the wife of Njǫrðr, although their union was not the happiest. Freyr married the beautiful Gerðr, daughter of the giant Gymir, for whose love, as we will see, he gave up his sword. Freyja married Odr, who, however, was always far away on the road and much neglected her.

One day, a seductive woman arrived in Asgard: Gullveig, a witch expert in sowing discord among the Gods. She soon corrupted with cupidity the minds of the Goddesses, the pillars of morality and honor. It was therefore decided to sentence the witch to death. Gullveig was part of the Vanir, who asked for his immediate return.

Odin knew that not listening to this warning would lead to war but the witch's behavior was punished. The Gods erected a funeral pyre, bound the witch there, and set her on fire but only after three attempts did the flames consume her body. The fire gave the Vanir a pretext to attack the Æsir.

Both factions fought furiously but the fate of the war remained in constant balance, bearing witness to mutual value. However, one day, using the strength of their magical arts, the Vanir managed to destroy the mighty walls of Asgard. Tired of a fratricidal war that had led to this ruin, the two families then signed a peace treaty and exchanged hostages. The Æsir sent Mimir and Hoenir to the Vanir, who handed over Njǫrðr, his son Freyr, and his daughter Freyja.

To seal their pact, the representatives of the Æsir and the Vanir then had a goatskin brought and spit in it, sealing the peace just stipulated. From this goatskin was born Kvasir—the wisest creature in the universe and living testimony of the divine agreements.

The truce was immediately put to the test by the Vanir. They often asked the wise Hoenir for advice but he agreed to answer only if he could consult with Mimir. One day, tired of always having to wait for the two Æsir to consult each other before speaking, the Vanir beheaded Mimir. Odin, full of contempt and pain, went to the realm of the Vanir, had the head of the God delivered to him, and returned to Asgard. He sprinkled it with magical herbs, interrupting the decomposition process and preserving its wisdom. Since then, in times of need, Odin often converses with Mimir's head, asking it for advice on what to do.

Asgard, the Realm of the Gods

Sacred is the earth that extends into the sky, home of the Æsir and the Álfar. It is furrowed by cosmic rivers, which make it difficult to pass from earth to divine fortresses unless one knows the appropriate runes to climb along the Bifrǫst bridge. The Yggdrasill ash pushes one of its roots up there, and the Urdarbrunnr spring stretches beneath it.

We do not know a specific name for the heavenly earth. Men call it Goðheimr, "world of the Gods," but perhaps its ancient name was Ásaheimr, "world of the Æsir."

At the center of the sky rises the rock of Asgard. There are the main divine sanctuaries and the salon of Valhalla. The twelve celestial kingdoms on which the dwellings of the Gods arise depend on it.

After completing the work of creation and establishing the Midgard, as we know, the sons of Borr (Odin, Vili, and Vé) built Valhalla.

The fortress was once protected by a wooden fence. However, this had been broken during the war against the Vanir and, for this reason, the Gods had subsequently built impregnable stone walls. Thus, the fortress of Asgard had arisen. There the Gods had gone to live with their families and the Irsir lineage had descended, destined to inhabit that fortress and all the heavenly kingdoms.

In the middle of Asgard lies Iðavǫllr, the vortex field. It is the place where the Gods met for the first time, at the beginning of the world, to undertake the construction of the fortress. In that place, the Vǫluspá states, they will meet again, after Ragnarök.

Ásgrind is called the gates of Asgard. Glaðsheimr is its first and main building. In it, there are the twelve seats of the Gods, plus the high throne of Odin. Made of pure gold, both inside and out, Glaðsheimr is reputed to be the largest and the best of the buildings ever built.

In Asgard, there is also the salon of Valhalla, where Odin welcomes the Einherjar.

There is also another building, Vingólf, the sanctuary of the Goddesses. It, too, is intended for the Einherjar. Some, however, identify him with Gimlé, a palace destined to resist the flames of Ragnarök and which will be the happy abode of all the right men who lived throughout the course of history.

As in Glaðsheimr, the throne of Odin dominates the twelve seats of the Æsir, so Asgard is surrounded by twelve celestial kingdoms, in which the Gods have raised their marvelous dwellings.

Himinbjǫrg, the "mountain of the sky," is the fortress that rises to the confines of the firmament, in the place where the leap of the Bifrǫst bridge is broken. The solicitous Heimdallr resides there, guarding the temples of Asgard, so that they do not have to violate the mountain giants. In his cozy home, Heimdallr drinks the good mjǫðr gladly. It is true that the lusty Loki suggested that Heimdallr's was not an attractive life, always a sentinel, in a bad climate, and with his back eternally wet with dew.

Valaskjálf, the "fortress of the fallen," is the palace that Odin erected for himself at the beginning of the days and that the Gods covered with silver. In that dwelling is the throne Hliðskjálf. When Odin is seated, he can observe everything that happens in the nine worlds, as if everything happens within walking distance of him. From that seat, he witnesses every man's behavior and understands everything he sees.

The world of clear elves, Álfheimr, is also in the sky, not far from the land of the Irsir. It was given to Freyr by the Gods, at the beginning of time, as a gift for his first tooth.

Fólkvangr, the "camp of the people," is the kingdom of Freyja. In that place is also Sessrúmnir, the room with "spacious benches." Here, Freyja decides the choice of places at the table for the fallen whom she herself chooses on the battlefields of the world. In fact, half of the Einherjar belongs to her, while the other half belongs to Odin.

Thor lives, with his family, in a place called Þrúðvangar, "fields of force," or rúðheimr, "house of force." There he built an imposing residence, Bilskírnir, "flash of light." Full of arcades, with its five hundred and forty [six hundred and forty] rooms, it is, together with Valhalla, the largest building ever built, among those covered by a roof. It is here that Thor returns, tired and with ragged clothes, sometimes even battered by his exploits.

Ýdalir, the "yew tree valley," is where Ullr raised a court for himself. In that place, Thor's stepson spends his time skiing along the snowy slopes and hunting wild animals with his bow.

Another splendid heavenly home is Søkkvabekkr, the palace with "submerged benches." It belongs to Sága and falls on cold waves. In that place, Odin and Sága meet to drink, day after day, happy, in gold cups.

Breiðablik, "ample splendor", is the place where Baldr built a dwelling for himself and his wife, Nanna. It is a place where nothing impure can exist and where there are very few evil runes.

Glitnir, the "scintillating," is the home where Forseti established his court. The walls and the jambs are of gold. The roof is, likewise, supported by golden columns and is covered with silver. Anyone accessing that place to resolve their conflicts is pacified.

Nóatún, the "fortress of the ships," is where Njǫrðr built his home and reigns happily in impressive sanctuaries. It is located on the seashore, where one can feel the seagulls swarming in the morning and smell the omnipresent aroma of algae. In that place, his children, Freyr and Freyja, came to Njǫrðr infinitely dear.

Among the divine kingdoms is also Þrymheimr, the fortress of the giant Þjazi, located between the peaks of Jotunheim. After the death of his treacherous lord, it was, in fact, inherited by his daughter, Skaði, the bright wife of Njǫrðr. She still lives in that indispensable place, where she skis for long stretches and goes with the bow in search of wild animals.

And then there is Fensalir, the "hall of the marshes," where Frigg lives with his maids.

Finally, there is a land without a name. It is wooded, dotted with bushes and tall grass. There does not appear to be any buildings or other dwellings there. Vidarr has lived there since he was a child and he spends his time riding proud foals.

Valhalla and Hel

Valhalla is an immense hall located in Asgard with Odin, its leader. The souls of half of those who had an honorable death in battle—better known as the Einherjar—will be led by Valkyries inside the hall. The other half will go to Fólkvangr, the Goddess Freyja's field.

The thought of every warrior at the moment before putting on his weapons and preparing for battle was dedicated to Valhalla. Each drove away the fear of death, which attacked even the bravest of warriors, thinking of the majestic building that stood out, luminous and inaccessible, up in the sky, among the abodes of the Gods, in Asgard. In Valhalla, it is impossible to see the opposite wall. The beams that supported the immense palace were made from the sharp spears of the most reckless warriors. The roof was then covered with shiny gold shields, finely decorated with scenes of war. The interior furnishings were made with the clothes of the soldiers who, until their last breath, had fought, disdainful of danger, in war.

In the middle of the room, a long fire burned, lined on both sides with benches. The place for a newcomer would never have been missed and the Valkyries quickly filled, a pity well beyond the limit, food plates and beer horns and the mead.

But only the bravest warriors, the einheriar, the "champions," could pass one of the five hundred and forty grandiose gates of Valhalla. From each of them, eight hundred warriors could pass, lined up shoulder to shoulder. It was at one of these entrances that one could watch the spectacle offered by a skilled juggler, capable of throwing seven solid-gold, razor-sharp swords into the air and then catching them on the fly.

The main door, however, the one destined for the warriors chosen by Odin himself and manned by him, was in the west. It was the Valgrind, a majestic hermetically closed gate with a magic formula. Before crossing the Valgrind, the deserving dead had to swim the river Thund, crossed by treacherous currents and whose fruits, breaking on sharp rocks, echoed darkly all around. The gate, then, was guarded by a ravenous wolf, an emblem of the ferocity of war, and by an eagle, mighty lady of the birds of prey, the bird warriors par excellence. Inside the building intended for them, the "champions" found a very large courtyard capable of accommodating the multitude of deaths produced by the innumerable wars that had broken out since the beginning of time.

When the banquet was over, when Odin retired, the heroes threw themselves on the straw-covered benches and slept until a golden rooster woke them up the next morning with his singing.

Upon waking, the mood was combative. The heroes chewed poisonous mushroom to provoke anger attacks and climbed on the benches. They brandished weapons and launched into furious fights on Ida's field.

They weren't really fake battles. On the contrary, every hero fought like a madman. At the end, the field was covered with head and limbs. In addition, the champions trained by improvising jousting rides, to prepare for the supreme and final battle that would take place at the end of time, when, together with Odin, they would be called to fight against the inhabitants of Muspelheim. However, when the bell was rung announcing lunch, everyone went to collect and rearrange the pieces of their bodies. Together, they crossed the wide doors of Valhalla, friends as before, preparing for a new, succulent feast.

Other essential characters of Valhalla were the Valkyries, "those who choose those killed in battle." Female semi-divinities, armed with shields and lances, invulnerable and immortal, the Valkyries rode in the air during battles, always at Odin's side, ready to collect the spirits of heroic fighters. In Valhalla, however, the extraordinary Amazons were the cupbearers of the champions, to whom they carried cups filled with frothy beer. The strident servants of the protected ones of Odin, and who were occasionally also their lovers, had names that recalled the warrior spirit. Thus was Urist, "the one who makes one tremble"; Skdguì, "furious"; Hild, "warrior"; Randgrindhr, "bearer of shields"; Geirahodh, "battle of spears"; Herfjótur, "bond of the hosts"; and Gdìl, "noisy." Although they had passed away, the warriors retained all their ravenous appetites and boundless thirsts. The multitude of heroes was fed daily by the chef Andhrímnir, who every day baked the boar Sæhrímnir, endowed with the astonishing power to resurrect each time at dawn, ready to be cooked again in the Eldhrímnir cauldron.

As a drink, the heroes, in addition to beer, sipped continuously on the mead that flowed in streams from Eikþyrnir's sterns, a gigantic goat that, resting on the roof of Valhalla, grazed the leaves of the Lóradhr pine, epigone of the ash of the world. The divine patron of the einheriar, the supreme Odin, instead fed exclusively on wine, an exquisite nectar prepared just for him. The throne of Odin was located in the northern part of Valhalla and it was there where the God sat to join the celebrations of his heroes, next to four of his sons: Týr, Hod, Vidar, and Vali, all Gods of war.

Those who were not considered worthy of enjoying training and mead in Valhalla after their deaths, who were stained with grave faults, or who had died of illness or ingloriously, were destined for the joyless world at the base of the nine worlds, in horrible underground depths dominated by Hel. The queen of the realm of the dead, like her father Loki, was a dual figure, with a face that was half-corpse and half-normal. She lived in a gloomy building whose doors were opposite the direction of the sun, devoid of any comfort, in which the name of each object was a symbol of misfortune. For example, his plate was called "Hunger," his knife "famine," and his bed "bed of death."

Hel was, therefore, the lowest realm of the nine worlds: a forgotten light, dark and frozen, photovoltaic in an impenetrable fog, perpetually whipped by the wind and beaten by the rains.

Its entrance was a dark and deep grotto, guarded by Garmr, a huge monstrous reed. No one could escape him and the death he represented, as evidenced by the clotted blood on the chest and face of the diabolical animal.

A dangerous road led all the way down. Along the way, the dead had to listen to the gruesome noises of the underground river Gyoll until they met a giantess on a bridge, from which they were then examined. This safety measure served to prevent access to the living—unwary, curious onlookers spying on the mysteries of the afterlife. After this bridge was the gateway to Hel, a symbol of entry into the world of the dead from which there could be no return.

The door was guarded by a rooster that would, with its chilling song, wake up the ranks of the dead and the lords of Hel, summoning them for the extreme battle that would see them in opposition to the Gods and the guests of Valhalla at the end of time.

Hel was divided into various environments, each with a different punishment and torment. At Naigrindr, night and day, the condemned were struck by a monstrous giant and forced by horrible female creatures to drink goat urine, with the image of the sweet mead served by the beautiful Valkyries in Valhalla in their minds.

On the beach of the dead, the place of torture destined for perjurers, murderers, and adulterers, the condemned were continually devoured and tormented by a dragon and many poisonous snakes. To reach this beach, the dead had to swim a river in which sharp knives and swords were shaken.

On this beach, a grotesque shipyard worked at full capacity. There, immersed in the stench of blood and excrement, monstrous creatures had the task of tearing the nails of their victims. The nails were, in fact, the material with which the ship Naglfar was built without ceasing. It would transport the infernal lords and sons of Hel to the war against the lords of Valhalla. Even today, in the Scandinavian countries, the habit of cutting the nails of the dead before burial is widespread, as if to slow down the process of building Naglfar.

This was also the place where, on an island in the middle of an underground lake, Fenrir, Odin's main enemy, was exiled and chained.

Norse Gods

Odin, Father of All the Gods

Son of the giant Borr and Bestla, the daughter of Bolþǫrn, Odin is the oldest of the Æsir. Born in ancient times, he and his brothers, Vili and Vé, were the creators of creation. They killed the primitive giant Ymir and, with his carcass, forged the earth and the sky. Then they regulated the course of the stars, established the computation of time, and founded the new universal order.

Odin is supreme among the Gods and governs all things in the world. Although the other Gods are also powerful, everyone serves him, as children do with their father. In fact, he is called Allfǫðr, "father of all," because he is the father of the Gods and of men, the creator of all that he has brought to completion with his power.

Odin resides in Asgard, in the silver palace called Valaskjálf, "fortress of the elect," which he himself raised. In that room is the throne Hliðskjálf, from which Odin observes the whole world and the conduct of every man, and understands all the things he sees.

Bride of Odin is Frigg, daughter of Fjǫrgynn, from whom he had his son Baldr and, perhaps, also the blind Höder. But first, Odin had his wife Jǫrð, who had given him the strongest and most powerful of his sons, the God of Thunder, Thor. His lover, Rindr, also gave him his son Váli, and the giantess Gríðr gave birth to Vidarr the Silent. Hermóðr is also called the son of Odin. In addition, the brave Týr is a son of Odin though some say that, rather, he is the son of the giant Hymir.

Odin had many lovers among the mortals, from whom he generated great heroes and important kings of kings.

The names and appellations with which Odin is known among the sons of men are very high, and no man has enough wisdom to know them all. It is said that in ancient times, in Asgard, he had twelve names. The first was Allfǫðr, the second Herjan, the third Hnikarr, the fourth Hnikuðr, the fifth Fjǫlnir, the sixth Óski, the seventh Ómi, the eighth Biflindi, the ninth Sviðurr, the tenth Sviðrir, the eleventh Viðrir, and the twelfth Jálkr.

He is also called Sigfǫðr and Valfǫðr because he establishes who should win and die in battle. His other names are Hangaguð, "God of the hanged," Haptaguð, "God of bonds," and Farmaguð, "God of loads."

There is another reason why all these names have been assigned to Odin: There are many languages in the world and all people turn to the God in their own language when they invoke or pray to him.

Hooded, or with a wide-brimmed hat on his head, Odin wanders through the worlds on his horse Sleipnir, which is the best of the steeds and has eight legs. He is accompanied by two wolves called Freki and Geri, the "greedy" and the "devourer," which eat the food on his table. It is said that Odin has no need for nourishment: Wine is, for him, both food and drink.

Two crows are perched on his shoulders and whisper in his ear all the things they see or hear. They are called Huginn and Muninn, "thought" and "memory." During the day, Odin makes them fly around the world; at mealtime, they come back and tell him what they knew, and Odin understands everything. This is why men also call him Hrafnaguð, "God of crows."

One cannot speak of Odin without mentioning his wisdom, the immense knowledge he possesses, as he is the oldest of the Gods and the creator of the world. He first learned all the arts and then the men learned them from him. Among the many names and epithets of Odin, several refer to the vastness and depth of his knowledge: Fjǫlnir and Fjǫlsviðr, "very wise," Sanngetall "[he who] senses the true," Saðr "[he who] speaks the truth," and, again, Forni, "ancient," that is, connoisseur of all things from their origin.

Odin knows not only the origin of all things, the mysteries of the nine worlds [nío heimar], the order of all lineages, and the beings that live there but, also, what has yet to happen. He knows the destiny of every man and the fate of the universe.

Odin loves to dispute with ancient and wise creatures. Under the guise of Gágnraðr, life was played by challenging the giant Vafþrúðnir, whose scholarship was renowned in all nine worlds and, after a series of questions about the past, the present, and the future of the world, to a race of wisdom. The giant answered promptly. Gágnraðr asked him what Odin had whispered in Baldr's ear before he was placed on the funeral pyre. At this point, Vafþrúðnir recognized Odin but by then had lost the game.

Another time, presenting himself as Gestumblindi, Odin challenged a king named Heiðrekr to a competition of riddles. After a series of questions that the king answered without difficulty, Odin asked him the same question he had already asked Vafþrúðnir. At that question, the king recognized the God and tried to kill him but Odin escaped by turning into a hawk.

Beside him, Odin holds the head of Mimir, which is, for him, an inexhaustible source of knowledge and which reveals to him much of the news from the other worlds.

Moreover, he himself has only one eye, having given the other to draw a sip of water at the source of wisdom in Mímisbrunnr. From that mutilation, the epithets of Bileygr ("one-eyed") and Báleygr ("flaming eye") were derived.

Odin's knowledge has another very important origin: He knows the secrets of the runes, those letters with angled lines, which, engraved on wood and stone, on sword blades, on the poet's tongue, on horses' hooves, on the palms of midwives, on the edges of the bridge, on the beer that is brewing, and on the amulets are the very origin of all knowledge and all power. Odin obtained this wisdom by sacrificing himself as a sacrifice to himself, as he himself told Loddfáfnir:

"Here, I know, I hung on the high trunk whipped by the wind for nine whole nights, wounded by a spear and given to Odin (myself sacrificed to myself)! On that tree that nobody knows from which roots it rises. I was hungry but nobody was there to give me bread; I was thirsty but no one handed me horns to drink. I looked down, screaming, got the runes up, and then fell out of there!"

In this way, Odin obtained the runes and dominated all his powers. Immediately, he felt like flowering internally, growing and becoming powerful. "Word for me from word, I came with the word! Work for me from the opera, I went with the work! "

It seems that the tree to which Odin hung itself was, indeed, the great ash tree Yggdrasill, which drew his name, "Yggr's steed," in memory of his sacrifice.

The whisperings of Ygdrassil had told Odin of the prophecies of Ragnarök. He knew of how Surtr would lead the giants in their war against the Gods and how he would set the earth on fire. Odin could not prevent this end but he hoped that, with wisdom, something of the Gods and men could be saved.

So, Odin, disguised as a greying old man, moved over the Bifrǫst Bridge towards Midgard and began searching for the Mimir well. The well was in the root of Ygdrassil in the Jotunheim. It was kept by Mimir, the man who drank its wisdom each morning and who kept watch over the horn, named Gjallar, that Heimdallr, the white watcher, would blow on the day of Ragnarök.

Odin traveled for many days and nights, meeting man and giants, challenging and being challenged. He discovered the location of the well and also the great price he had to pay for its waters: For anyone who would drink, Mimir asked for the right eye. After many days of travel, he came to the edge of the well.

And so Mimir took up his horn Gjallar, filled it with the water from the well, and gave it to Odin.

Odin took the horn and drank deeply. His eyes opened and he saw the great and horrible sufferings that would strike both men and Gods: Ragnarök, the reasons and causes, and why they must be.

He drank twice and saw the ways that Gods and men—with noble courage—fight and defeat the evils. He also saw his death and the death of Fenrir. He saw how Thor would succumb to the venom of Jörmungandr, and how Loki would fight against Heimdall. He saw his own death, devoured by Fenrir, and many more deaths that would come of Ragnarök.

After he saw these things, Odin, with his hand on his face, removed his right eye. Mimir took it and threw it into the well as a sign to any who might pass of the price that Odin paid for his wisdom.

Then Odin returned to Asgard on his throne, considering the things he had seen.

The wisdom of Odin is knowledge, magic, and poetry at the same time. It is not only dry erudition but also the source of its powers. He practices his arts with the runes or with those magic songs called galdrar, so that he himself and all the Æsir are also called "smiths of songs." But there are songs—certainly not within the reach of the sons of men—that only Odin knows and that give him immense power not only over things and elements but also over the will and feelings of men. Nine spells, the most terrible, he learned from his maternal uncle, the son of Bǫlþorn.

We know some of these songs because they were heard when Odin himself referred them to Loddfáfnir.

With his spells, Odin knows how to tie the soul and the will of men. They can quell hatred and contention, quiet anxiety and sadness, and even cure illnesses. On the other hand, he knows how to bring misfortune, sickness, and death to men. He knows how to remove a man's wisdom or strength to transfer them to another. This kind of magic, which Odin knows well, is called seiðr and practicing it involves shameful attitudes for males—so much so that it has long been handed down only among the priestesses.

Odin knows how to seduce women by arousing love in their hearts, and not even the most shrewd young girl resists him, because he knows how to fascinate her, bending her feelings to his will. It is the God himself who says this: "I know this: If I wish to have the love of a girl, however wise she may be, I bend the woman's white arms and distort all her thoughts."

If the fire burns, Odin knows the words to turn it off. If there is a storm at sea, Odin chants the wind according to his will and calms the waves. "This I know: If I see the high hall burning around my companions at the banquet, the fire does not burn with such ardor that I cannot extinguish it by singing my spell. And I still know this: If I find myself in difficulty to save my ship on the waves, the wind I calm on the waves and fall asleep all over the sea."

Odin cannot be imprisoned or tied. He knows songs that untie knots, that make the chains fall from his wrists and jump the logs from the feet. He has the power to change his appearance so that nobody recognizes him until he wants to keep the unknown. While his body lies as if dead or asleep, Odin becomes a bird or an animal, a fish or a snake, traveling to distant lands in the blink of an eye to take care of their own affairs ... or those of others.

Odin knows where all the treasures of the world are hidden, and he knows the songs that open the earth and the rocks, stones and mounds, that bind those who live there with words, and then enter and take whatever they like. He raises the dead from the earth, or sits by the gallows and unties the tongues of the hanging men, who report their knowledge to him. Therefore, he is called lord of the spirits of the dead and hanged. "I know this: If I see a hanging man on a tree at the top, I engrave and paint runes so that the man walks with me and answers my questions."

If Odin sees witches fly in the night, he knows how to confuse them and dispel them: "I know this. If I see the 'horse riders' playing games in the air, I can make them lose their return to their bodies at home, to their spirits at home."

Many names were given to Odin in commemoration of his witchcraft abilities: Ginnarr, "deceiver," Glapsviðr, "able to enchant," Gapþrosnir, "magician," Gǫndlir, "[he who] possesses the magic rod," Haptaguð, "God of ties," Skollvaldr, "powerful in deception," and Svipall, "changeable." He transmitted most of his faculties to his priests, who were close to him in wisdom and magical practices. But with the passage of time, others also learned a lot and gave rise to a magical practice that spread in the northern countries and lasted a long time.

Odin states that he always spoke in verse. It is also said that it was he who started the art of poetry in northern Europe.

Odin is, indeed, the lord of poetry, which is a supernatural power not far from the same magic, because between the qualities of poet, vate, prophet, and magician there is no substantial difference. Odin took away from the giant Suttungr the sacred mead that makes poets of those who drink it, and who now cherishes himself. It is said that Odin poured part of that mead onto the earth, giving human beings the priceless gift of singing.

Odin is also a God of war. He is called Sigfǫðr, "father of victory," because he decides to whom the victory in battle should go, and Valfǫðr, "father of the chosen ones," because all his children are his adoptive sons. With these two names, Odin distributes victory and death in battle: both gifts appreciated by warriors.

Odin fights with his magic arts and takes pleasure in the feast of wolves and crows. Many of his epithets recall this bellicose aspect: Gǫllnir, "[he who] is in the noise," Atriðr, "[he who] advances riding," and Fráríðr, "[he who] rides to [the battle]."

The infallible spear that he holds in his hand, and that was given to him by the dwarves, is called Gungnir. Runes are engraved on its tip. With that spear, he initiated the first world war, the conflict between Æsir and Vanir. Since then, on the eve of battles, he has turned it towards the host to whom he has decreed defeat. He is, therefore, called Dresvarpr, "[the one who] hurls the spear," Geirloðnir, "[he who] invites with the spear," and Biflindi, "[he who] shakes," implied, the spear. Odin also possesses a helmet of gold, so that he is called Hjálmberi, "[he who] wears the helmet."

Odin looks terrible to enemies, as he is an expert in the art of changing shape and color at will. He has, in war, the power to blind, deafen, or terrorize his enemies, to unleash terror in the ranks, to render weapons incapable of hurting like mere twigs. No one can throw a spear so hard into the fray that Odin can't stop it with a single glance. His warrior abilities have a magical basis, as they stem from his knowledge of runes and spells. "I know that," said Odin to Loddfáfnir, "if I have great urgency to chain my enemies, I will check the blades of my adversaries, rendering their swords and their clubs useless."

On the other hand, he himself chooses whom to protect in the fray, to make his devoted warriors invulnerable. He can make those who descend into battle come out of it safe and sound. "And I still know this: If I have to lead my friends in battle, I sing under their shields, and they go victorious to the fray and from the fray return safe and sound."

Odin establishes the fate of warriors. He gives them victory and decides when they should die. The devoted warriors trust him and invoke him as Sigfǫðr, "father of victory," Sigtýr, "God of victory," Sigþrór, "profitable in victory," Sigðir, "servant of victory," Sigtryggr, "faithful in victory," Sigrhǫfunðr, "prince of victory," and "Sigmundr," protector of victory." Tradition reports many examples of warriors who raised sacrifices and invocations to Odin to achieve success in battle.

For the elect of God to obtain victory or to die gloriously are two equally desirable things. In fact, the fate of those who die in clashes, who are, in all respects, the "chosen ones" of the God, is not sad. In fact, this term is called the fallen in battle: that is, "chosen." Odin welcomes them as his adopted children and assigns them to the classroom of Valhalla, where they participate in the eternal banquet over which he presides. Odin is, therefore, also invoked as Valfǫðr, "father of the fallen," Valtýr, "God of the fallen," Valþǫgnir, "[he who] welcomes the fallen," and so on. To a seer awakened from the realm of the dead, Odin presents himself as the son of Valtamr, "used [to the choice] of the fallen," and this, too, is indeed his name.

It is precisely in this way, by establishing to whom death will occur on the battlefields of the world, that Odin chooses his champions, the ones who will form the ranks of the Einherjar, the warriors destined to fight alongside him on the day of Ragnarök. They form the army of souls that rides in the sky on stormy nights. As their leader, Odin is called Herfǫðr and Herjafǫðr, "father of the hosts," Hertýr, "God of the hosts," Herjan, "leader of the hosts," and Herteitr, "happy in the ranks."

Linked to the cult of Odin are the congregations of ecstatic warriors, the úlfheðnar and berserker, the "werewolves" and the "bear clothes," which, before the battle, entered a state of fury, called berserksgangr, in which they began to growl, drool, and bite the edges of their shields. Then they threw themselves screaming into battle, swirling swords and axes, and making emptiness all around, insensitive to pain and fatigue. Later, they collapsed to the ground, exhausted.

With a hat on his head and a cloak over his shoulders, sometimes holding on to his spear like a stick, Odin wanders the streets of the world. Thus, he is also called Vegtamr, "wayfarer," Gagnráðr, "[he who] knows the way," and Kjalarr, "[he who goes on the] sledge."

Odin moves along the streets like a pilgrim, disguising his appearance and his real nature. Therefore, he is called Grímr and Grímnir, "masked," as well as Hǫttr, "hooded," Síðhǫttr, "well hooded," Lǫndungr "[the one who wears] the bristly coat," and Hrani, "unkempt." He generally appears as a mature or elderly man with a long beard, for which reason he is called Hárbarðr, "gray beard," Langbarðr, "long beard," Síðgrani, "well maned," Síðskeggr, "well bearded," and Hengikeptr, "wrinkled cheek."

Odin is, indeed, the God of travelers and of all those who move along the roads. During his travels, he asks for hospitality for the night, both in the rulers' houses and in the homes of the humble. He is also called Gestr, "guest." In fact, in every stranger welcomed into the house, the same Odin could be hidden in disguise. Woe to those who do not wait for the sacred duties of hospitality!

Under the name of Grímnir, Odin came as a guest to King Geirrøðr, who, suspiciously, cruelly tortured him by keeping him chained between two blazing fires. After revealing the secrets of the divine world and some of his numerous epithets, Odin finally revealed his true identity to him. King Geirrøðr ran to free him but tripped over his sword and fell, stabbed.

Thus, Odin assumed the name of Jálkr when he was a guest with the people of Ásmundr; Gagnráðr when he went to compete on remote knowledge with the giant Vafþrúðnir; Sviðurr and Sviðrir at SøkkMimir, son of Miðvitnir, whom he killed; Bǫlverkr near the giant Suttungr; Hárbarðr when he had an exchange of insults with Thor; and Gǫndlir when he presented himself incognito in the presence of the same Gods. Many of Odin's names are, therefore, tied to specific vicissitudes. In truth, it is a great and wise person who knows with certainty all these stories.

Odin's appearances are a theme dear to the Nordic tradition. The sagas report many witnesses who, for one reason or another, encountered a disturbing-looking wayfarer along the way, which presented itself with one or the other name. Sometimes he knocked on the doors of houses, asking for hospitality for the night. Those who had to deal with this mysterious wayfarer realized that it was an uncommon individual but only at the time of his leaving, or even later, did they sense that they had dealt with Odin.

Often, Odin intervened in the lives of sovereigns and heroes, causing their births, helping them on various occasions, and, eventually, bringing them to death. This is the case, first of all, with the Vǫlsungar lineage, which was said to descend from Odin himself and which the God followed carefully for many generations until excellent heroes such as Sigmundr, Sinfjǫtli, Helgi, and Sigurd came from that lineage. On many occasions, Odin was at their side, helping them in every way and giving them wise advice. However, at the right moment, he came to claim their lives. It was Odin who showed up on the boat to claim Sinfjǫtli's body from his father's arms, and it was also Odin who personally supplied the spear with which Dagr could kill Helgi. Presenting himself with the name of Hnikarr, "[he who] instigates the battle," the God seduced the infuriated sea before Sigurd's ship but it was always he who provoked the disagreements and asperities that led to the death of the young hero and the ruin of his lineage.

This is just one example among many. On another occasion, Odin appeared, under the name of Hǫttr, "hooded," in the presence of the beautiful Geirhildr and arranged for her to become the wife of King Alrekr. Later, he helped the woman prepare an excellent beer for a competition and asked her instead "what was between her and the cauldron"—that is, the child she was carrying. Víkarr was, therefore, born already consecrated to the God, who made him a hero and an excellent sovereign. But then, as another story goes, Odin returned with the name of Hrosshársgrani ,"with a mustache like horsehair," and asked for Víkarr's death. A false hanging was staged. It was hoped that this would satisfy the God but it unexpectedly turned into a real sacrifice and Víkarr died, hanged and pierced by a rod magically transformed into a spear.

It is still told, in the saga in his honor, that the famous Danish King Hrólfr Kraki was hosted, during a trip to Sweden, by a mysterious farmer named Hrani. When, on his return, he refused certain gifts that he offered him, his fate was marked.

To Oddr, also a protagonist of a saga, Odin appeared under the false name of Jólfr. He gave him three magic stone arrows with which the young hero could kill a demon.

This happened naturally in pagan times. However, appearances of the God are recorded even after the conversion of the northern lands to Christianity. A historical saga tells of how the crew of a vessel took on board a hollow man, wrapped in a dark blue cloak, who said his name was Rauðgrani. He taught men the pagan creed and invited them to make sacrifices to the Gods. Eventually, a Christian priest became furious and hit him on the head with a crucifix. The man fell overboard and never came back. Although the saga does not expressly say so, the man was Odin.

It is said that, under the name of Gestr, Odin visited Óláfr Tryggvason, King of Norway (995-1000). The God presented himself in the guise of an old, hooded man, gifted, endowed with great wisdom and experience, who reported stories from all the countries of the world. The strange individual had a long conversation with the king. Then, at bedtime, he left. The next morning, the king looked for him but the old man had disappeared. However, he had left a large quantity of meat for the king's feast. King Óláfr, who was a Christian, forbade the eating of the food, because he had recognized Odin under the guise of a mysterious guest.

With the same name as Gestr, Odin appeared again, a few years later, in the presence of King Óláfr II Haraldsson the Holy (1015-1028). He came to the king's court in the form of a proud and unkind man. He wore a wide-brimmed hat that hid his face, and he had a long beard. During an interview, Gestr described to Óláfr the figure of a sovereign of past times, who was so wise that speaking in poetry was as easy for him as it was for other men to speak. He triumphed in every battle and could grant the victory to others, as well as himself, provided that he was invoked. From these words, King Óláfr recognized Odin and chased him away.

Bragi

Among the Æsir there is a God called Bragi. He is the son of Odin and possesses vast wisdom. Runes are carved on his tongue, and perhaps this is why he is so eloquent in speaking. He is even more skilled in the art of poetry, of which he is said to be the creator. From its name stems the skaldic art called bragr; a man or woman who possesses, to the maximum degree, dominion over the word is called a bragi. Equipped with a long and thick beard, he knows all the kenningars and poetic metaphors by heart, and explained them to Irgir during a banquet, without hiding from him the myths and stories from which they had originated.

Bragi's wife is Iðunn, the Goddess who guards the apples of youth. Bragi has children and also adopted children.

He is certainly not a warrior. Bragi, although he appears proud when necessary and claims to be ready to fight with anyone, prefers to calm tempers rather than exacerbate them. When Loki insulted him, at irgir's court, calling him a coward, he preferred to quiet the situation by giving him a horse, a sword, and a bracelet. But since the other did not cease provoking him, Bragi declared, in no uncertain terms, that he would have cut off his head had they not been guests in the hall of the marine giant.

On the other hand, despite not being a fighter, Bragi attends Valhalla, where, together with Hermóðr, he welcomes the renowned sovereigns who fall in battle.

Loki

Loki is a central figure in the development of many Norse myths. The shrewd God of cunning and chaos, an ingenious master of deception, skilled in double speech, more than a divine figure, he is the personification of fraudulent cunning and the subtle art of deception.

A solitary figure among the men who populate Norse spirituality, Loki is an ambiguous character for several reasons. His name is linked to fire, an element connected to both civilization and destruction. Although included among the Æsir Gods, he is related to the giants, symbols of chaos; however, the "shame of the Ases" will be defined more than once, a deceiver with the desire to subtly destroy the assigned order. In some myths, he is the faithful companion of Odin and Thor, who are often saved by his cunning.

Loki is, therefore, not referred to as an evil God in an absolute sense. He alternately helps Gods and giants according to whose line of action is most pleasant and advantageous for him at that time. He knows and embraces the principle of the male, inflicting Asgard with his lies, but defends and preserves the principle of good to maintain the balance of opposites until the end of time. His presence is, then, fundamental because this man must necessarily oppose the good.

Loki has physical traits of exceptional beauty, which, at the same time, inspire admiration and fear, a sign of the ambiguity that characterizes him. He is the son of the giants Farbauti, "cruel attack," and Laufey, "leafy island" but he made a pact of alliance with Odin, playing on the roots of the giant blood of the Father of the Gods, being included among the Æsir.

Being of uncertain sexual boundaries, he is famous for having given birth to a progeny of ruthless beings, evil instruments whose only purpose is destruction and death. However, he also generated Sleipnir, Odin's trusty and fast horse.

He is the father of Angrbodha, the giant prostitute who was condemned to the stake for her crimes. When her body was reduced to ashes, Loki, entranced by the spectacle of death he had witnessed, took his daughter's heart, which mysteriously survived the flames, and devoured it. The evil heart, fruit of his own blood, fertilized its father, who later gave birth to three monstrous creatures: a wolf, a great snake, and a girl. All three were raised in Jotunheim until Odin discovered the deception. Presuming their danger, the father of the Gods ordered them to be brought before him so that he could decide how to neutralize them. The progeny of Loki would prove to be as evil as, if not more than, their father.

The wolf would become the mammoth Fenrir. Initially, the Gods kept him with them but the fierce animal grew more and more, in size, ferocity, and intelligence—so much so that only the God Týr, known for his courage, dared to feed him. Eventually, the wolf became too great a danger and the Gods decided to bind him. Fenrir will remain a prisoner until the day of Ragnarök, when he will be released and avenged by devouring Odin.

The snake was, instead, exiled in the oceanic abysses, where it grew out of all proportions. Its coils became so long and powerful that it could hold the Earth in an indissoluble grip. It will rise from the waters during Ragnarök, corrupting the whole world with its poison. Then it will face Thor, by whom it will be killed. However, the God of Thunder will die soon after, killed by his poison.

The girl, who came to the world the first time that the disease struck humanity, became, for men, the symbol of despair and pain. Her name is Hel. Horrible to look at, perpetually poised between life and death, between rebirth and putrefaction, she always looks downwards, to indicate the earth, depository of corpses. Hel was exiled to the deepest bowels of the Earth and the Gods made her the horrifying lady of the underworld. However, she was satisfied and, as a thank-you, gave the ravens Huginn and Muninn to Odin. Odin, therefore, gave her the authority to manage the penalties and torments to be given to all those whom Valhalla had not accepted. Hel became queen of the dead without honor due to illness, accident, or old age, traitors, cowards, and criminals.

Loki incurred a tremendous punishment for having caused, among other misdeeds, the death of the God Baldr. He was led to a cave in Niflheim and the Gods turned one of his sons into a ravenous wolf, which was then pushed to devour another of his children. With the guts of the torn child, a rope was then forged, used to tie Loki to three pointed stones. A snake, suspended above his head, perpetually trickled poison into his face and burned him constantly if Sigyn, his devoted wife, did not pick up the poisonous drops in a basin. However, when the basin was full and she had to move away to empty it, the devastating poison burned Loki's face, making him scream and shake. His jerks were so violent that they caused earthquakes.

Loki will remain in this state until the day of Ragnarök, when he will free himself and line up alongside the giants in the ranks of evil. He will finally fight the guardian of the rainbow, Heimdall, in a battle that will see them both die.

Thor

Thor, the eldest son of Odin and Jordh, Goddess of the Earth, is the God of Thunder and Storms, the defender of Asgard, constantly engaged in fighting giants and performing extraordinary deeds. These characteristics of the forced protector of the Gods against monstrous beings led him to assume the appearance of Hercules in the interpretation of Tacitus.

Thor is a formidable warrior, the strongest of the Ases, and has three treasures: iron gloves, a belt that doubles his power, and the hammer Mjölnir, which has the power to return after being thrown.

The perpetually frowning face of the God is framed by a long, dark red beard and long reddish hair, and his eyes are the same color as the burning embers. Thunder is the noise that heralds his coming, provoked by the wheels of his chariot, pulled by two goats, Tanngnjostr and Tanngrisnir. Once, driven by hunger, he killed them to eat them but made them come back to life simply by placing his hammer on their skins.

The peasants worship him as the husband of Sif, Goddess of Fertility. In addition, his hammer is the symbol of the lightning that precedes the rains, vital for the crops. Thor lives with his bride in the largest palace in Asgard but has numerous relationships with human women and giantesses.

During Ragnarök, he will fight against the snake of the world, one of the daughters of Loki. He will succeed in killing the snake but he will die shortly afterward due to his injuries.

Týr

Týr, son of Odin and Frigg, is the God of Wisdom, War, and Law. Originally, he was the most important and powerful God—a role assumed in the Norse era by Odin.

He is the God to whom the warriors turn before battle, the tutelary deity of a just victory to whom one asks for protection. He is not the God of an exasperated and brutal confrontation but, rather, the protector of war understood as the last solution. He is, therefore, also the God of law and justice, seen not as a conciliation of the parties but as an armed clash. As in a court, in fact, the duelists follow a code and undertake to recognize the outcome of the dispute. The winner is on the side of reason, and Týr writes the sentence with the blood of the defeated.

Like Odin, Týr lost a part of his body, his right hand. Fenrir, wolf son of the God Loki, had become too great a danger to the Gods, who decided to chain him. However, such was the strength and cunning of Fenrir that he twice managed to free himself from the chains that imprisoned him. Odin then decided, making use of the magic arts of the dwarf artisans, to prepare a magical lace, fragile but capable of imprisoning even the strongest being, and challenged Fenrir to get rid of it. The wolf, astute as his father, accepted the challenge on the condition that one of the Gods put a hand in his jaws while he was chained. Týr did not hesitate. However, when the attempts to get rid of Fenrir failed, he lost his hand, cut by the wolf's sharp teeth. Yet Týr's sacrifice allowed the Gods to chain Fenrir to a rock and place a sword between his jaws to torture him as he tried to break free.

At the end of time, Týr, already the victim of a wolf, will be killed by Garmr, the guardian dog of the underworld.

Baldr

Baldr is the most beautiful and purest God of heart, the favorite son of Odin and Frigg, loved and respected by every living creature. His heart has never been affected by the baseness and wickedness that sometimes find a place among the other Gods. In his gestures and in his words, neither arrogance nor self-satisfaction is ever perceived but only a boundless modesty. Because of the envy of the other Gods, his advice, always matured with serenity and knowledge, is never heard.

His mother, Frigg, knew that he was destined for an early death and traveled all over the universe trying to find a way to prevent him from grabbing his demise. He then gathered all the plants, animals, and elements of creation, imposing on them a universal oath: Never would anything or anyone harm Baldr. Enthusiastic about the news of his invulnerability, the Gods started to throw him any object, certain that nothing could harm him. Loki, always envious of good Baldr, turned into a mortal woman and spoke with Frigg, succeeding in deceiving him to discover the weak point of the oath.

Loki picked up a mistletoe plant and approached Höder, Baldr's blind brother, who had kept to himself. Stating that he wanted to help him participate in the game, Loki gave Höder the mistletoe plant, now like an arrow, and helped him aim. The plant was then thrown towards Baldr, piercing and killing him.

From this story, we understand that Baldr represents the embodiment of pure innocence, betrayed by the wickedness of others—a mythical projection of the pessimism that characterizes the vision of the world in the Nordic culture.

The Gods asked the queen of the underworld to return Baldr's life to him but she set a condition: All the beings of the earth, alive or dead, had to cry, showing, indeed, the universal pain over his death. Only Loki, cowardly assuming the features of an old hag, did not cry, condemning Baldr to remain in the realm of the dead. One of the names by which Baldr is best known, which best sums up the tragedy of his whole existence, is "God of tears."

Heimdall

Heimdall is the keeper of Asgard and Bifrǫst, the rainbow bridge that connects heaven and earth, Asgard with Midhgard, which men can admire only after storms. His sister is Sif, the wife of Thor.

The reason for the relationship with Sif is not very clear. It is said that, in fact, Heimdallr was the son of nine different mothers and not of one, while his father was Odin, in turn, Thor's father.

It is said of Heimdallr that he is a shining God of light and that he is also a valiant soldier and an expert warrior

He watches tirelessly and, like Odin, has received great power by depriving himself of a part of his body: He cut and buried one of his ears under Yggdrasil, receiving, in exchange, very fine sight and hearing. Heimdall is capable of sensing every threat in the universe.

He is the owner of the Gjallarhorn magic horn, with which he can call and warn the Gods in the event of an attack. During Ragnarök, this horn will resound, grave and penetrating, in all nine worlds, calling to the final clash the forces of good against those of evil. Heimdall will witness the collapse of Bifrǫst, shattered by the destroyers of the universe, and will fight against Loki. He will succeed in killing Loki and will still play his horn for a last, short time before dying from the wounds he has sustained, with the image of the end of the universe imprinted in his eyes.

Two creatures that accompany Heimdallr are the golden cock Gullinkamb, which has the task of waking Odin's soldiers every morning to incite them to battle, and the golden horse Gultopp.

Vidarr

Vidar, the second strongest Æsir after Thor, is the son of Odin and the giantess Gríðr. He lives in Asgard in the peaceful hall Vidi, with a great garden. He is known for being silent and at peace with nature in his garden, working on a special shoe.

This shoe is the strongest existing shoe and is made from all the scraps and pieces of leather trashed in Midgard. Vidar will use this special shoe at Ragnarök to avenge his father's death, placing one foot on Fenris's lower jaw and using his hands on the upper jaw until Fenris's mouth tears apart.

Forseti

Forseti, the son of Nanna and Baldr, is the law-speaker and the God of justice. Most of the time, he is the judge who decides the outcome of a dispute between the Gods. He applies the fairest judgment. Sometimes he spends his day in the practice of meditation.

Freyr

Freyr, one of the most beautiful Gods, is the God of fertility, prosperity, wealth, and harvest. Member of the Vanir, he is the son of Njǫrðr. Freyr has a twin sister named Freyja and is married to the giantess Gerðr. On the day of Ragnarök, Freyr will pay for this love with his life.

Often, he uses his chariot, conveyed by his boar, named Gullinbursti, to travel long distances.

Hermod

Hermod is the son of Odin and Frigg. When Baldr was killed, he was the one to ride to Hel and try to bring Baldr back from the realm of dead.

Njǫrðr

Njǫrðr is the God of the wind. He is a Vanir and is the father of Freyja and Freyr. Njǫrðr is married to the giantess Skadi.

Mimir

Mimir is the God of knowledge and wisdom. During the war between the Æsir and Vanir, Mimir was sent to the Vanir. However, the Vanir beheaded Mimir and sent his head back to Asgard. Odin, to retain Mimir's wisdom, preserved his head with magic so that he can provide his knowledge.

Norse Goddesses

Iðunn

Iðunn is the Goddess of youth, the one who has the gift of preventing the death and aging of all the Gods (or Æsir, according to Norse mythology). It is said that she and her spouse, Bragi, God of poetry and adviser of Odin, had acquired this power through special medical knowledge. However, in later periods, the myth said that the power of Iðunn resides in some magical apples she alone possesses, as the only cultivator. The Goddess, therefore, has the task of continually supplying these apples to the other Gods, who, eating regularly, will remain young forever. The most famous myth relating to Iðunn is her kidnapping by the giant Þjazi.

Iðunn is represented as a beautiful woman, looking like a 20-year-old girl or even a teenager, sometimes with loose blond hair and sometimes with hair tied in two long braids. She holds an apple basket.

Bragi, her husband, is depicted as a man with a very long beard, always intent on playing the harp, a symbol of poetry.

According to some legends, Iðunn's apples also have the ability to give fertility. For this reason, she is also referred to as the Nordic Goddess of fertility, like the Goddesses Freyja and Sif. In fact, Iðunn has some features in common with these two Goddesses. Sif has long golden hair, while Freyja is often represented with flowers in her hair or as a creature of the woods. There is no lack of paintings and illustrations that see her together with two cats, a symbol of Freyja but also of the Goddess Frigg, wife of Odin.

Freyja

Freyja is the Goddess of love but is also associated with lust, fertility, sex, and war. She lives on Fólkvangr, the "camp of the people" and is the daughter of Njǫrðr. She has a twin, Freyr, and is married to the God Odr. With him, she has two children: Hnoss and Gersemi.

Despite being a Vanir, she became an honorable member of the Æsir after the end of the war between the Æsir and Vanir.

She is said to have a beautiful appearance and long golden hair and is often represented as having a wild, sylvan appearance, wearing a dress made of flowers (or sometimes a green dress) and surrounded by animals. She is desired not just among the Gods and Goddesses but also among giants and dwarves. She loves jewelry and fine materials and has quite often used her beauty to get what she desires. She owns the necklace known as Brísingamen.

Freyja loves to travel with her chariot, pulled by two cats. She is also able to fly with her cloak of falcon feathers. Freyja has a boar named Hildisvini, which she rides when she is not using her chariot.

Her marriage to Odr is said to be very happy, although he is often absent from home, leaving his bride in tears made of gold.

It is not certain, however, if Freyja is faithful to him, as the other Gods—especially Loki—often accused her of being lustful.

Sif

Sif is the Goddess of grain and fertility. She has long, beautiful, golden hair and is married to Thor. She has a son named Ullr. Loki once cut her golden hair while Sif was sleeping. He was then forced by Thor to replace the hair.

Frigg

Frigg is the Goddess of love, marriage, fertility, and motherhood. She is the queen of Asgard and the wife of Odin. They have two sons: Baldr and Höder. She is the stepmother of Bragi, Heimdall, Hermod, Höder, Týr, Vidar, Thor, and Vali. Equipped with the same intelligence as Odin, Frigg also has the gift of foresight, which she uses to predict marriages and births. Along with her husband, she is also the protector of all manual arts and crafts—above all, traditionally feminine arts, such as weaving, which is said to have been personally handed down to all women.

The origin of another symbol of hers—namely, the bunch of keys—is not known. It was said that Frigg always kept a bunch of keys but the myth that explains the reason for this has been lost over time. One explanation is that the keys represent the Goddess's ability to open the doors of unknown worlds, increasing her knowledge or ability to see the future.

She is the only one permitted to sit on Odin's high seat, "Hlidskjalf," and look out over the universe.

Her three handmaids are Fulla, Gná, and Hlín. The first, always next to the mistress, has the task of serving her and assisting her inside the domestic walls, and, in particular, in the Fensalir, Frigg's personal home within Asgard. Hlín has the task of acting as an ambassador and carrying messages from the Goddess to the earth under the guise of a hawk. Gná fulfills some of Fulla's duties and some of Hlín's duties.

Fulla is the most important of the three. She is depicted with long hair, always at Frigg's feet, very often holding a casket, as it was believed that one of her most important tasks is to carefully fold her mistress's stockings or shoes. Frigg and Fulla are sacred winter, especially the days immediately after the solstice, during which the girls are forbidden to spin as a sign of respect to the queen of the Gods. Fulla, in addition to being a maid, is also Frigg's confidante and keeper of her secrets.

The ability of the maiden Hlín to transform herself into a hawk derives from a cloak woven with hawk feathers—perhaps by Frigg herself. This cloak has the property of making anyone who wears it capable of flying.

Ragnarök

In Norse mythology, Ragnarök is the event that marks the end of time. The Gods will fight with the giants in a battle in which both will die and the sky and the earth will burn after the final war between good and evil. There is nothing the Gods can do to prevent it. Ragnarök is also the means by which the purified universe can begin a new cosmic cycle. It is, therefore, a cyclical end of the world, followed by a new creation, followed in turn by another Ragnarök, and so on, for all eternity. In other words, creation and destruction are like points at opposite ends of a circle; one cannot reach one without meeting the other.

The first sign that heralds Ragnarök is the death of Baldr. Killed by Loki and forced to remain in the realm of the dead, he obliges the Gods to face the fact that they cannot escape their fate. Despite their divine character, they are, in fact, subject to the same fate as human beings: They, too, must die. However, this awareness does not lead to resignation. Even if their actions are in vain against the destiny that awaits them, Odin and the other Gods will still gather the most skilled warriors for the final battle against the giants.

The second sign is the end of civilization and order in the realm of men. Men will have forgotten their traditions, ignored kinship ties, caused fratricidal wars, and abandoned themselves to a profound nihilism. Depravation will remain the only ideal of mankind. Fathers will kill their own sons, while mothers will seduce them. Brothers will sleep with their sisters.

Then a terrible winter (knows as Fimbulvetr) will come, which will not give way to summer for three years. Torrential rains, wind, and dreadful snowfall will torment the globe, covering it with a thick and impenetrable blanket of frost.

The third and final signal is the disappearance of the sun (known as Sól) and the moon (known as Máni). The Skoll and Hati wolves, which have been chasing them since the beginning of time, will be able to reach and devour them, depriving the world of light and plunging the Earth into eternal darkness. At the same time, all the stars will burn and fall from the firmament, making sailors wander in the immensity of the oceans where every light has now disappeared.

The war will therefore begin….

Three roosters will announce the beginning of Ragnarök. One will warn the giants in Jotunheim, another the dead of Hel. The cock Víðópnir, from the top of Yggdrasil, will warn the Gods. The great tree, which contains the Nine Worlds in its branches and roots, will tremble, shaking the universe with terrible earthquakes that will tear the Earth apart and destroy whole mountains.

At that point, all the chains will break. Loki and his son Fenrir, the great wolf, will free themselves from their long captivity and wander the world, sowing death and destruction. Even the serpent of the world, Jormungandr, son of Loki, so far confined to the ocean depths, will re-emerge from the waters, causing tidal waves, flooding valleys, submerging cities, and drowning thousands of defenseless men.

The infernal ship Naglfar, the vessel built with the nails of the condemned in the kingdom of the underworld, will leave the beach of the dead to transport the army of evil.

Fenrir will advance with wide-open jaws. He will have become so huge and evil that his upper jaw will touch the sky while his lower jaw will rest on the earth, destroying everything he encounters. Jormungandr, his brother, the serpent of the world, will eventually take his side, spreading so much venom that he poisons the whole Earth.

Led by Surtr, the giant who sweeps the Earth with his huge flaming sword, the sinister inhabitants of Muspellsheim will advance from the south, leaving behind them a hell of flames, and will reach Bifrǫst, the rainbow bridge that leads to Asgard, which will collapse underneath their weight. Preparing for the final battle, the lords of terror will reach the plain of Vigrid, where they will meet their natural allies: Loki, who has escaped his imprisonment, along with his monstrous sons and all those who had been exiled and imprisoned in the dark recesses of Hel. All the evil of the universe will gather in that place.

At the same time, Heimdall, guardian of Asgard and Bifrǫst, will leave Himinbjorg, his hall, and will summon the Gods with his horn, without stopping. It is a signal that the Gods know well, warning that the war has begun and that their destiny is calling them.

Odin, grim-faced but with fire in his eyes, will wear his helmet and, holding his terrible spear, will mount Sleipnir and summon his champions, the indomitable warriors of Valhalla, whose loyalty and courage have not been affected, even by death. The newly assembled army, an immense expanse of swords and armor, will greet the father of the Gods, who will advance, together with all his sons, to the battlefield that destiny has established for them. There is no fear in their eyes. They know that this is the war that will put an end to all the battles, in which all the heroes of the Norse pantheon will fight side by side against the giants and all the evil creatures present in the universe. Their only desire is to fight valiantly to the end.

Odin has no doubts. He immediately aims at the most terrible enemy, the ravenous Fenrir, who awaits him threateningly, showing him huge open jaws, a hell of sharp teeth. Thor, beside him, will be unable to help Odin because he will be attacked by Jormungandr. Thus, Fenrir will prevail over the father of the Gods, who will be imprisoned between his jaws and devoured. Vidar, one of Odin's sons, blinded by anger, will face the beast and, pressing one foot on the lower jaw and grasping the upper jaw, will shatter the wolf's head, tearing it and avenging his father.

Freyr will fight against Surtr and will perish for giving his sword to his servant and messenger, Skirnir.

Thor, making his way, with the deadly blows of his hammer, between the ranks of the giants, will face his long-time enemy, Jormungandr, who is so big that he encircles the terrestrial globe. The strength of the God is incredible. After a long battle, he will succeed in smashing the head of the hated snake, which will vanish into the depths of the sea from which he appeared. However, weakened by the evil poison, after having taken the hammer and made nine steps, the God of Thunder will collapse to the ground, devoid of life. The same fate will befall Týr, engaged in an unequal struggle against the horrendous mastiff guarding Hel. At the end of his strength, he will be able to beat the mastiff to death before expiring.

The last duel will be between Heimdall and Loki, who will kill each other. Before dying, Heimdall will succeed in playing his horn for the last time, then will collapse on the fiery battlefield with the image of the end of the universe imprinted in his eyes. The guardian of the rainbow will be the last warrior to close his eyes forever that day.

Many Gods will succumb and Surtr, by now the uncontested master of the field, will burn the Earth and make the nine worlds fall into a hell of flames, transforming the whole universe into a huge incandescent sphere and purifying it of all the evil committed that day.

Finally, in the final reversal of the original process of creation, the Earth, now devastated by the most destructive war in the history of the universe, will sink into the boiling sea, slowly disappearing under the waves. Suddenly, there will be only darkness and the perfect silence of the empty before creation.

The Ginnungagap will once again reign.

... and a New Beginning

Good and have evil clashed and, together, they died. There are no winners in Ragnarök. Fire has the purifying role necessary to allow rebirth. For a new world to be born, in fact, the old one must first be destroyed.

It is predetermined that when the major part of the Gods and giants have died, a new world will be reborn from its ashes: A new, boundless Earth will emerge from the water, beautiful and green. The eagles will fly again and the wheat will return to ripen in fields that have never before been cultivated.

Before the battle of Ragnarök, a man (Liftrasir) and a woman (Lif) will take refuge in the sacred tree of Yggdrasil. When the battle is over, they will come out to see the new world. The two will eat only morning dew drops and will populate the Earth again with numerous offspring, becoming the creators of a new human lineage.

Some Gods will survive: Vidar, the son of Odin, who killed Fenrir while avenging his father; his brother Vali; the two sons of Thor (Modi and Magni), who will inherit the hammer of their father; and Baldr and his blind brother, Höder, who will return from the kingdom of the dead.

With the rebirth of the world after Ragnarök, the golden age of the Norse Gods will return.

The survivors will go to Idavoll, the shining plain on which Asgard formerly stood. Together, they will build their splendid new homes there.

Baldr will find that, among the grass of the new lawns, even the chess pieces of the Gods have disappeared.

The noble warriors who had fought alongside the Gods during Ragnarök, who died for the good of humanity, will continue to live in the joy of the halls of Gimle, the new heavenly home, where they will drink excellent mead.

Meanwhile, in Nastrond, the "shore of corpses," the wicked will stay in an immense building, devoid of any beauty, whose walls will be formed by snakes that will pour their poison into the river flowing through the hall. Finally, though the wolf Skoll had deprived the world of light because he had managed to devour Sól, the beautiful child positioned to drive the chariot of the sun, she died before giving birth to a beautiful daughter, who will travel the same sky, thus finally bringing light and warmth to the new world.

CHAPTER 4: NORSE TALES

The Deception of King Gylfi

King Gylfi ruled the land of Svíþjóð. It is said that he gave a beggar, as a reward for having entertained him, land in his kingdom that four oxen could plow in a day and a night.

She was a woman of the Æsir lineage, and her name was Gefjun. Odin, who at the time ruled over the Danmǫrk, had sent her to Svíþjóð in search of new territories. As soon as Gylfi gave her his promise, Gefjun went north, to Jotunheim, and there he begat four sons from a giant. He turned them into oxen and yoked them to the plow. The plow excavated with such force and so profoundly that it melted an enormous tract of land, which the oxen dragged to the west, over the sea, placing it in a narrow.

Gefjun gave the land the name of Sjóland and settled there after having built the Danmǫrk. During the reign of King Gylfi, Lake Lǫgrinn was formed where the land had been turned from the plow, in the Svíþjóð. In fact, there are as many bays in Linngr as there are headlands in Sjóland.

King Gylfi was wise and knew much magic. He was impressed by the power of the Æsir and wondered whether this power depended on their nature or whether it had been given to them by the Gods they worshiped. Therefore, he embarked on a journey to Asgard, the seat of the Gods. So that he wouldn't be recognized, he disguised himself as an old man.

But the Æsir were wiser than he, as they had the gift of foresight. They learned of his journey even before he arrived and prepared sjónhverfingar to confuse him.

When Gylfi entered the citadel, he saw a building so high that the top could hardly be seen. The roof was covered with golden shields placed like tiles, just as the poets said that the hall of Valhalla was made. In the doorway was a man who juggled daggers, keeping seven of them in the air at the same time. He asked Gylfi what his name was. Gylfi replied that his name was Gangleri and that he had sought asylum for the night when he came from far away. He also asked who the dwelling belonged to. The man replied that it belonged to their king and made way for Gylfi so that the traveler could enter the skáli.

As he walked through the doors, Gylfi reminded himself of the ancient saying:

"All doors, before crossing them, must be spied on. They must be scrutinized. What a doubt it is every time where the enemies sit in the hall [that is] in front of you."

As soon as Gylfi was in the skáli, the door closed behind him. Inside there was a large crowd: those who played, those who drank, those who fought. Gylfi looked around. Much of what he saw seemed incredible.

At the bottom of the skáli stood three tall thrones, one above the other, and on each sat a man. Gylfi asked for the names of those leaders. The man who had brought him there told him that whoever was sitting on the lowest seat was the king and his name was Hár, "tall." The neighboring one was called Jafnhár, "just as tall," and the one on the highest seat was Þriði, "third."

Hár asked the newcomer if he had many commitments. Otherwise, he was free, like all the others, to eat and drink in the great room. Gylfi wanted to know if there was any sage present there, and Hár replied that he would not leave that place if he had not been made wiser before. He said, "Go ahead while you ask; sit must he who speaks."

King Gylfi asked many questions about the origin and the end of the world and about the Gods and their stories. The three mysterious rulers answered all his questions. It was a long and beautiful story in which the three sages of Asgard revealed the entirety of Nordic wisdom to King Gylfi.

At the end of the long narrative, Hár said, "Now, if you want to know something more, I don't know how you can do it, because I haven't heard anyone say more about the history of the world. Do all this to know the use you want."

Soon after, Gylfi heard a great rumble of thunder. He looked around and realized that he was on level ground. Around him, he saw neither the skáli nor the great palace he had entered.

Then he set out on his journey and returned home to his kingdom, telling all that he had seen and heard. After him, these stories were handed down from father to son.

The Building of Asgard and the Birth of Sleipnir

A very interesting story concerns the reconstruction of the wall around Asgard. After the Vanir had succeeded in breaking the citadel's defenses, the Gods were worried that someone might besiege and conquer their home

One day, an artisan came to the Æsir and offered to quickly build a stone stronghold around the citadel, so solid and well made, he said, that it would resist the action of the most powerful giants. In exchange for his work, he demanded the Goddess Freyja, and also to take the sun and the moon.

The Gods gathered in þing to discuss the proposal.

The craftsman belonged to the lineage of the jotnar. The Æsir, obviously, had no desire to strip the sky of the sun and the moon, nor to send the splendid Freyja into the Jotunheim.

After talked with each other for a long time, the Gods judged the offer to be very tempting but regarded the required reward as excessive. The Æsir told the craftsman that he would have what he had asked for only if he had completed the construction in half the time established. He would work all winter but if, on the first day of summer, some part of the fortress had been unfinished, he would have lost all rights to the reward. Furthermore, he had to do the work alone, without receiving help from anyone. The Æsir believed that, under such conditions, the jǫtunn would never be able to complete the work and that, with the arrival of summer, they would have liquidated the builder and found themselves with a good part of the work already completed.

The craftsman agreed, provided he was allowed to get help from his horse, Svaðilfǿri. The Æsir wondered if there was some trap in this request. Loki acted as an intermediary between the two parties and proposed to the Gods that they accept the condition. The craftsman, who was a jǫtunn and did not feel comfortable in the midst of the Æsir (especially if Thor returned, as in those days he was in the east, fighting the trolls), demanded, after many oaths, that the Gods guarantee him safety for as long as he remained with them. They committed themselves to honoring the agreement if the terms were respected.

The craftsman began his work on the first day of winter. In a short time, the walls of Asgard began to grow visibly. During the night, Svaðilfǿri transported a large number of stones to the construction sites. To the Æsir, it seemed extraordinary how great and heavy those stones were. It seemed to them that half of the work was done by the mighty steed. As the winter progressed, the Gods began to worry. They had signed their agreements with solemn oaths and incontrovertible testimonies and they could not hold back if the junntunn had concluded his part of work in the established time.

As winter slowly came to an end, the construction of the fortress advanced at a fast pace. The walls were so high and solid that no one would ever succeed in conquering them. When there were only three days left in the early summer, the construction of the fortress had almost reached the gates. Then the Æsir called a new assembly during which they asked each other how they could have accepted such a disastrous pact. Who could have advised delivering Freyja to the jotnar and destroying the sky by depriving him of the sun and moon? It was clear that this advice had come out of Loki's mouth, which had always been the cause of the worst ailments. The Gods attacked him and told him that they would condemn him to a terrible death unless he made sure the craftsman lost the right to compensation. Frightened by the threats, Loki swore that he would see to it that the artisan did not fulfill his commitments.

On the same night, while Svaðilfǿri was pulling a large number of stones towards the fortress, under the watchful and satisfied eye of the craftsman, a mare came out of the woods and neighed several times.

When the stallion noticed that it was a mare, he became angry. In vain, the craftsman tried to hold him back. Svaðilfǿri broke the reins and chased the mare into the forest.

The two horses chased each other all night. Despite his desperate efforts, the craftsman lost track of them. At dawn, he returned sadly to the fortress, stared at it, and immediately realized that he would no longer be able to complete it by the appointed time. He was then taken by the jǫtunmOdr, the fury of the giants, and rushed against the Gods. So, the Æsir invoked Thor. He appeared immediately, spinning Mjölnir. It was the sound of hammering, and certainly not the sun and the moon, which paid the compensation due to the craftsman. At the first blow, he shattered his skull into a thousand pieces and sank it under the Niflhel. A short time later, leaving the semblance of the mare, Loki returned to Asgard. He had behaved in such a way with Svaðilfǿri that he later gave birth to a colt.

The pony was gray and had eight legs. He was very fast, and no other steed could keep up with him. He was named Sleipnir and became the usual mount of Odin. He was considered the best horse existing between the Gods and men, and many wonderful steeds descended from him.

The Gifts of the Dvergar

One day, as a joke or out of malice, Loki cut Sif's hair. When Thor noticed, he seized Loki and would have smashed all his bones if Loki had not promised to immediately go to the Svartálfar and have a crown of gold forged by Sif.

This is the reason why, even today, poets talk about the gold "hair of Sif." Then went Loki from those dvergar, called Ívaldasynir, sons of Ívaldi, and they forged three wonderful treasures. The first was the golden hair, which would stick to the skin as soon as it was placed on Sif's head and which was able to grow like hair. The second was the Skíðblaðnir ship, whose sails, once unfurled, were immediately filled with a breeze that pushed the ship along any route one wanted to direct it. Furthermore, if desired, the ship could be folded like a tablecloth and placed in a bag. The third treasure was a spear, Gungnir, which always hit the target when it was launched.

Later, Loki, boasting of the three treasures forged by Ivaldi's sons, bet his head with a dvergr named Brokkr that his brother, Eitri, could not have built three objects of equal value.

Arriving in the workshop, Eitri threw a pigskin into the forge and ordered Brokkr to blow the bellows continuously until he ordered him to stop. Eitri had just left when an insect landed on Brokkr's hand, stinging it. However, following his brother's orders, Brokkr did not stop for a moment and continued to wind until Eitri came to pull a marvelous pig with golden bristles out of the forge.

Immediately afterward, Eitri put on the gold furnace and gave his brother the same task. Brokkr began to handle the bellows and did not stop even when the insect came to sting his neck painfully. He blew without pause until Eitri removed a wonderful gold ring from the furnace.

Finally, Eitri introduced into the iron furnace and, once again, told Brokkr to blow with the bellows. The work would be completely useless, he said, if he stopped for even a moment. Brokkr set to work but, this time, the insect landed between his eyes and stung him so fiercely that blood ran down his face. Seeing nothing, Brokkr left the bellows and tried to catch the fly. Upon his arrival, Eitri was afraid that the work was ruined. He took a hammer from the forge and noticed, with disappointment, that the handle was too short.

However, he gave the objects to Brokkr and told him to go and dissolve the bet.

The Æsir sat on the seats of the council to judge which objects were most precious—whether those forged by Ívaldasynir or those brought by Brokkr.

Loki first presented the treasures commissioned from Ívaldasynir. He gave Sif the golden hair, Freyr the ship Skíðblaðnir, and Odin the Gungnir lance, illustrating the virtues of each object.

Then Brokkr presented his gifts. He gave Odin the Draupnir ring, saying that every nine nights there would be eight rings of equal weight. He gave the pig Gullinbursti to Freyr, explaining that he could run both in the air and in the water, at night or during the day, like any steed. Moreover, he added, no night was so deep, no place so dark, that it would not be illuminated by its golden bristles. Finally, he handed the hammer Mjölnir to Thor, explaining that with it, he could hit any opponent as hard as he wanted, without the hammer being damaged or broken. Moreover, he said, if he threw it at an enemy, he would never lose it. Mjǫllnir, in fact, had the virtue of returning to him, however far he could throw it. If desired, he could even shrink that hammer to such an extent that he could slip it into the collar of his shirt.

"The only flaw," he concluded, "is that the handle is a little short."

The Æsir, after reflecting, said that the hammer Mjǫllnir was the best of all the treasures, as it would allow them to defend themselves from the jotnar and the other giants. Thus, they established that Brokkr had won the bet.

Immediately, Loki offered to redeem his head. However, the dvergr replied that this was not in the pacts.

"Take me, then!" yelled Loki and fled. In fact, he wore a pair of shoes that allowed him to run even in the air and on the water. Brokkr asked Thor to capture him, and he brought back Loki without missing a beat.

Then Brokkr stepped forward, determined to cut off Loki's head. However, Loki retorted that he had committed only his head. The neck was not part of the agreement. Exasperated, the dwarf decided to sew his mouth. He grabbed a knife to pierce his lips but the blade couldn't cut into the meat. Then Brokkr summoned his brother Eitri's awl. Immediately, the instrument appeared in his hand. With that, he could drill holes in Loki's lips. Having done this, Brokkr sewed the mouth of the áss with a special hoop called Vartari.

Later, however, Loki removed the points.

The Sons of Loki: Jormungandr, Hel, Fenrir, and the hand of Týr

A giantess lived in Jotunheim; her name was Angrboða. Loki found his heart, half-roasted, among the ashes and devoured it. He was made pregnant and, when his time came, gave birth to three children. The first was a wolf named Fenrir. The second was a snake named Jormungandr. The third, a girl, had a half fresh and rosy face, and a half bruised and withered face. Her name was Hel.

But when the Æsir learned of these three monstrous sons who were raised in the Jotunheim, they threw the lot, and the prophecies announced that only misfortune and pain would come from them. It seemed obvious that such monstrous progeny announced great evils, given the nature of their mother and, above all, their father.

Then Odin sent the Gods to the Jotunheim to take the three brothers and had them taken with him. When this tremendous sonship came before him, he took the serpent first and threw it into the uthaf, the outer ocean that surrounds all the lands. However, the icy waters had a life-giving effect on Jormungandr. The serpent grew so much that it ended up encircling the whole world and, having found its own tail in front of it, clasped it between its jaws, encircling the lands in an enormous living circle. It was called Miðgarðsormr, the "serpent of Midgard."

Then Odin turned his attention to Hel. He threw her into the Niflheimr and allowed her to build the dark house of Éljúðnir there. He gave her power over the nine worlds so that she became the lady of all those who died of illness or old age. Hel became the Goddess of the dead.

As for Fenrir, the prophecies said he was destined to cause serious misfortunes in the future and even that he would become the slayer of Odin. The Gods had such respect for their homes and sanctuaries that they never wanted to stain them with the blood of the wolf. Thus, they saved Fenrir's life and allowed him to be raised in Asgard.

However, as he grew older, the wolf Fenrir became a huge and ferocious beast, so much so that only Týr had the courage to approach him to offer food. The Æsir began to be afraid of him, knowing the terrible prophecies concerning him. Finally, they decided to bind him to prevent him from doing harm.

The Æsir forged a very strong chain, which they called Løðingr. But how to approach Fenrir to be able to tie him? A ruse was urgent. Thus, they showed the chain to the wolf and proposed, as a challenge, that he prove his strength against it. The wolf looked at the chain, which did not seem, to him, to be beyond his own strength. He let himself be tied up. Then, with a minimum of effort, he broke Løðingr and freed himself.

However, the Æsir did not give up. They forged a second chain, more resistant than the first, and called it Drómi. They took it to the wolf and proposed that he try it. They said that he would have great fame if he could free himself from a chain made with so much mastery.

Fenrir sniffed it. The chain seemed pretty tough but it was also true that Fenrir's strength had grown a lot since he had broken Løðingr. After all, he reflected, no fame was obtained without facing dangers. He let himself be chained. Then he shook himself, kicked, and stirred. The fragments of the chain flew around him. So, he escaped from Drómi.

After this, the Æsir feared that there was no way to bind Fenrir. Odin then sent Skírnir, Freyr's messenger, down to Svartálfaheimr, to some very skilled dwarves, to forge a new chain. They gave him a lace called Gleipnir. It was thin and soft like a silk ribbon but almost impossible to break. It was made of six things: a cat's noise, a woman's beard, a rock's root, a bear's tendons, a fish's breath, and a bird's milk. And, in fact, this is the reason why, from that day on, women no longer grew beards, the leap of the cat no longer made any sound, and there were no longer roots under the rocks.

When Gleipnir was taken to the Æsir, they thanked Skírnir for his service. Then they went to the Ámsvartnir lake, on the islet of Lyngvi. Summoning Fenrir, they showed him the lace and proposed that he try to break it, warning him that it was much more resistant than it appeared from its appearance. The Gods passed it to each other, testing it with the strength of their own hands, and it did not tear. However, they were sure that the wolf would succeed without effort.

"I will not get any glory by tearing such a thin piece to pieces," Fenrir said. "But if it is as resistant as you say, it means that it is made with malice and deceit, and it will never tie my paws."

"Breaking this silk ribbon will be a joke for you, who has succeeded in shattering strong iron chains!" replied the Æsir. "But don't worry. If you fail to get rid of such a thin strip, you will not fear us anymore, so we will free you."

"I believe that if I could not free myself, it would be a long time before you came to my rescue," said the wolf. "I'm against being tied up with this ribbon. However, I have never stood back from a challenge. Rather, instead of challenging my courage, some of you must put your hands in my jaws to guarantee that all this is done without any deception."

The Æsir looked at each other. No one wanted to comply with Fenrir's request. Then Týr stepped forward and boldly stretched out his right hand between the wolf's teeth. Fenrir was tied up and began to experiment. However, the more he shook and kicked, the more Gleipnir tightened around his body, until the wolf was reduced to impotence. Then all the Gods laughed—except Týr, who lost his hand.

When the Æsir saw that Fenrir was completely immobilized, they took the rope sticking out of the tape, called Gelgja, and tied it around a heavy boulder, called Gjǫll, which was planted in the ground. Then they took a large stone, called Þviti, and used it as a picket, driving the boulder into the depths of the earth. During the whole operation, the wolf opened its jaws, trying to bite them. Therefore, the Gods put a sword in his mouth, with the hilt against the lower jaw and the tip against the palate, forcing him to keep his jaws open. Then they left him there.

Since then, Fenrir has howled horribly and from his mouth comes a trickle of drool mixed with blood, which flows away and forms the river Ván. He will remain so until Ragnarök.

The Kidnapping of Iðunn and Skaði's Marriage

Once upon a time, there was a giant called Ǫlvaldi. His lover was Greip, daughter of the giant Geirrøðr. Ǫlvaldi was very rich and possessed large quantities of gold. When he died, his three sons came to share the inheritance. To establish the exact amount of gold they would each receive, they decided that their mouths would be filled in turn, and so they did. The first among them was Þjazi, the second was Iði, and the third was Gangr.

Þjazi was a powerful giant. He lived in Þrymheimr, a fortress set between imposing mountains, and had two daughters: Mǫrn and Skaði.

One day, three Æsir left Asgard and set off. They were Odin, Loki, and Hønir. They climbed along mountain roads and traveled through desolate lands. It was not easy to find food in those lands, and soon the three began to feel hunger pangs. Finally, they came to a valley where a herd of oxen grazed. They took one, killed it, and prepared the seyðir to cook it. When a reasonable time had passed, they discovered the improvised rural oven but realized, with amazement, that the meat was not cooked yet. They waited a little longer, impatient, and Loki blew a long time on the fire to revive it. But when they looked back into the seyðir again, the food was not yet ready.

Then the three Æsir talked among themselves, trying to understand what that miracle meant. They understood that evil forces were at work. At that moment, they heard a murmur coming from the oak that rose just above them. They looked up and saw, perched in the branches, an eagle, certainly not small.

"I made sure that the meat in your seyðir wouldn't cook!" the animal explained. "But if you give me a portion of the ox, your food will be ready immediately."

The three Æsir agreed, and Odin begged Loki to divide the food into four parts. The latter agreed, though reluctantly, and divided the ox into quarters. Then the eagle sank down from the oak, grabbed both thighs and both shoulders and, once again, perched on the tree, where he devoured the whole animal. Loki took a long stick and, reaching upwards, hit the bird of prey between his shoulders.

The eagle took flight, with the club stuck to its back. Loki could not remove his hands from the other end of the stick. In an instant, the ax was lifted from the ground and soon Loki found himself so high that his feet hit the rocky peaks of the mountains and the tops of the trees. Soon his arms began to hurt so much that they seemed to want to break away from the trunk.

Loki shouted and repeatedly begged the eagle to give him respite, allowing him to return to the ground. However, the bird of prey was flying even higher, mocking him. Eventually, the bird told him that he would never let him go unless he swore to give him the Goddess Iðunn and her apples. Loki had to consent. Once the promise was obtained, the eagle returned to land and let him go.

Loki returned to his companions and together they resumed their journey.

Sometime later, once the three Æsir had returned to Asgard, Loki went to Iðunn and told her that he had found particular apples in a forest but he was not sure if he could guess the properties. He, therefore, asked her to go with him to observe them. Loki insisted that she carry with her a box of her precious apples, so as to compare them with those he had seen.

Iðunn had no reason to doubt Loki's good intentions. She followed him out of Asgard to a forest. From there, they crossed the Brunnakr streams to a stone fence that was the domain of Þjazi.

Others say, instead, that an eagle grabbed the Goddess in her claws and disappeared with her in the clouds. The raptor was the giant Þjazi who, with a single blow, took possession of the Goddess and the apples of youth that she kept.

The giants, inhabitants of the mountains, were very pleased when they saw Þjazi coming from the south, bringing with him Iðunn and the casket of her precious fruits.

For the Æsir, Iðunn's loss was a serious matter because, without her apples, they began to age. Their hair became white and their reflexes slow. They gathered in þing and asked each other what had happened to Iðunn. They discovered that the Goddess had last been seen in the company of Loki, and that she had left Asgard with him. They went to get Loki and took him to the ing. Then they threatened him with torture and death if he did not reveal his misdeeds and say how much he knew. Loki confessed what had happened.

"Your tricks, they will twist themselves against you!" cried Thor, furious. "Unless you bring back the wonderful girl, the one who nourishes the joy of the Gods!"

Frightened, Loki agreed to go to Jotunheim in search of Iðunn if Freyja lent him her hawkish disguise. He took flight and went north, to the land of the jotnar, in search of the Goddess.

After a long trek, he happened to Þrymheimr, the abode of Þjazi. It so happened that on that day, the landlord had gone out to sea, to fish, and had left Iðunn alone. Loki was able to enter the giant's fortress, where he found the young ásynja.

Immediately, he transformed Iðunn into a walnut and, squeezing it tightly between his claws, took flight, heading towards Asgard.

When Þjazi returned home and noticed Iðunn's appearance, it didn't take him long to realize what had happened. He put on his eagle disguise and threw himself in pursuit of Loki. Þjazi was far more adept at flying and created with his wings a great noise and whirlwinds of wind, in an attempt to embarrass Loki.

The Æsir saw from afar the hawk approaching as fast as he could, with the walnut clasped in his claws. He was chased by a large eagle. It was not difficult to understand that it was the giant who had kidnapped Iðunn. The

Gods placed a large pile of wood shavings under the walls of Asgard, waited for the hawk to penetrate the fortress, and then set fire to the pyre. A blaze of flames rose into the sky. Others say that the Gods fired fiery arrows at Þjazi. It does not matter. The feathers of the eagle caught fire and the giant fell ruinously inside the walls of Asgard.

The Æsir killed Þjazi inside the gates of Asgard. This is a very famous story. However, who was precisely to give him the mortal blow is not clear. Later, Thor stated, talking to Hárbarðr, that he was the one who killed him.

When Skaði, Þjazi's daughter, learned that the Æsir had killed her father, she put on a helmet and armor and, fully armed, went to Asgard, determined to get revenge. The Æsir, not wanting to get into a feud with Þjazi 's lineage, proposed that they be reconciled with them and offered her compensation. To begin with, they said, she could take a husband among the Gods. She was asked to choose her man by judging him from the feet.

Skaði examined the bare feet of the Gods for a long time. When he saw a couple of extraordinarily beautiful feet, she thought they were those of Baldr and said, "I choose this man! Little is bad in him!" But those feet belonged to Njǫrðr, polished by the sea and the waves.

Another condition that Skaði required to make peace was that the Æsir had to succeed in making her laugh, which she considered impossible. Loki intervened. He tied a rope to the beard of a goat. He tied the other end to his scrotum. Then he and the little goat pulled a little on one side and a little on the other, both screaming. Finally, Loki let himself fall at Skaði's feet, and she laughed. Thus, peace was made between her and the Æsir.

So, Skaði married Njǫrðr but their marriage didn't turn out very well. The woman loved the mountains and wanted to live in the homes that had once belonged to her father, in Þrymheimr. Njǫrðr, instead, wanted to live in his house by the sea, in Nóatún. So they decided to stay nine nights in Mrymheimr and the other nine in Nóatún but never to the satisfaction of either.

Since then, Skaði, the pure bride of the Gods, has lived in Rymheimr, in the homes of her old father Þjazi. In those places, she is happy. She walks for long stretches on untouched snow and hunts wild animals.

Kvasir and the Mead of Poetry

Of Kvasir, it was said that no one could ask him a question, whatever the argument, for which he did not have an answer ready. The origin of this great wisdom was well known: When the war between Æsir and Vanir came to an end, the two divine lineages celebrated their reconciliation by popping into a vase. From those spits, the Æsir s had created Kvasir, a living sign of friendship and peace, in human form.

Kvasir wandered around the world for a long time, bringing wisdom to human beings.

One day, he came to some dvergar, Fjalarr and Galarr, who offered him hospitality and invited him into the house to talk. Then they killed him. They poured his blood into two vessels, called Són and Boðn, and in a bucket, Odrørir. They mixed the honey with blood and obtained that mjǫðr, or mead, which makes the drinker a poet. The dvergar then told the Æsir that Kvasir had drowned in his own knowledge, as no one was wise enough to draw on his knowledge.

He came later to the Fjalarr and Galarr, a jǫtunn, in the name of Gillingr, along with his wife. The two dvergar invited Gillingr to sail on the sea with them but when they were far enough off the ground, they rowed against the rocks and turned the boat upside down. Gillingr could not swim and drowned. Fjalarr and Galarr returned to the boat and rowed towards land.

To Gillingr's wife, the two dvergar recounted what had happened. She began to weep in pain. Irritated by this harrowing lament, Fjalarr asked the giantess if she would be relieved to come and see the place where Gillingr had drowned. He invited her to follow him. Galarr, in agreement with his brother, climbed above the door of their home and, when Gillingr's wife came out, dropped a millstone on her head.

When Suttungr, son of Gillingr, became aware of this crime, he went to Fjalarr and Galarr, grabbed them, took them overboard, and abandoned them on a certain rock, which he knew would soon be submerged by the high tide.

The two evil dvergar pleaded with Suttungr to spare their lives and offered him the precious mjǫðr. And so it was agreed between them. Suttungr brought the mead home. He hid it in a place called Hnitbjǫrg, the "welded mountain," and placed his daughter Gunnlǫð on guard.

Traveling around the world, Odin came to a field where nine people were harvesting hay. He asked if their scythes needed to be sharpened. The workers agreed. Then Odin drew a whetstone from his belt and sharpened the blades. The ærælar tried the scythes; it seemed to them that they cut the hay much better than before. They then asked to be able to buy the whetstone.

Odin replied that he was willing to sell it but that whoever wanted to buy it should have set up a feast. Each of the ærælar declared himself willing and invited Odin to sell him the whetstone. Then Odin threw it into the air. They all started to grab it. They fought so much that, with the scythes, they cut each other's necks.

Later, looking for shelter for the night, Odin turned to a jǫtunn named Baugi, who was Suttungr's brother. Baugi complained about his situation. He told Odin that his nine workers had killed each other and that he had no hope of finding other workers to harvest hay for him. Odin said he was called Bǫlverkr and told Baugi that he would do the work of nine men. As a reward, he asked for a sip of Suttungr's mjǫðr.

Baugi replied that he had no mead, as Suttungr kept it only for himself but he promised that he would go with Blverkr and try to get it.

So it was that during the summer, the mysterious Bǫlverkr did the work of nine men. When winter came, he returned to Baugi and asked for his reward.

Both then went to Suttungr. Baugi explained to his brother the pact he had made with Bverlverkr and asked him if he could not give him a sip of mjǫðr. Suttungr replied that Baugi had no right to promise something that did not belong to him and refused to give him a single drop of the precious mead.

Bǫlverkr then told Baugi that they had to prepare a plan to take over the mead and Baugi agreed.

They went to Mount Hnitbjǫrg, near the cave where Suttungr had hidden the mjǫðr. Bǫlverkr drew a drill called Rati and told Baugi to drill the rock.

The junntunn set to work and, after a while, said that the rock was pierced. However, Balverkr blew into the hole and the splinters shot into his face. He realized that Baugi wanted to deceive him and told him to drill to the end. Baugi got back to work. When Bǫlverkr blew for the second time, the fragments fell inside.

Bǫlverkr then took the form of a snake and crawled into the hole. Immediately, Baugi tried to stick him with the drill but he missed.

The snake slipped to the place where Gunnlǫð was guarding the mjǫðr of Suttungr. After that, Bǫlverkr resumed his appearance. With the deceiving arts in which he was an expert, he seduced Gunnlunnð and lay with her for three nights.

Satisfied, the girl sat Bǫlverkr on the golden throne and allowed him to drink three sips of the precious mjǫðr. But he gave her a bad reward in exchange for his generous heart, in exchange for his sorrowful spirit. With a sip, Bǫlverkr emptied the Odrørir bucket. With another sip, he dried the Boðni jar. With a third sip, he drained the Són vase.

And once he had drunk all the mjǫðr, Bǫlverkr took the form of an eagle and flew off as quickly as he could.

When Suttungr saw the eagle take flight, he immediately understood what had happened. He, too, turned into an eagle and flew after him.

Suspended on his wings, Odin despaired of being able to reach Asgard. As they saw him coming, the Æsir s rushed pots out of their court. Flying over them, Odin spat into the mjǫðr. However, he could not save all the precious liquid, for Suttungr, also transformed into a bird of prey, was rapidly approaching.

Odin had to move away and, in his haste, he dropped a bit of mjǫðr from the beak. That quantity could no longer be recovered.

The next day, the hrímþursar entered Asgard and went to Odin's hall. They asked him about the mysterious Bǫlverkr. They wanted to know what had happened to him. Had he returned to the Gods? Or had Suttungr killed him?

Odin claimed that he knew nothing and swore on his ring. It is likely that the giants did not believe him.

In this way, Odin stole his mjǫðr from Suttungr and Gunnlǫð cried deeply.

Thor, the Undead Goats, and Skrýmir

After having yoked his goats Tanngnjóstr and Tanngrisnir to the wagon, Thor set out on his journey. Loki accompanied him.

After traveling all day, at dusk, Thor and Loki arrived at a farmer's house (they say his name was Egill), where they received lodging for the night. In the evening, Thor killed his goats, which were then skinned and roasted in the cauldron. When they were cooked, Thor sat down to dinner. He did not fail to invite the farmer, his wife, and their children to eat. The son of the factor was called Þjálfi, while the daughter was called Rǫskva.

Thor removed the skins of the goats from the fire and recommended that everyone throw the bones over it without breaking them. However, Þjálfi etched the femur of one of the two goats with a knife and broke it to suck the marrow.

Thor spent the night at the farmer's house. In the hour before dawn, he got up, got dressed, and, taking the hammer Mjölnir, made it spin and imposed it on the skins of the goats. The animals immediately got up, alive and well again, though Thor noticed that one of them limped. He realized that the farmer, or one of his family members, had ignored his recommendation. He became furious. Thor frowned and squeezed the hammer so hard that his knuckles turned white. As soon as the farmer saw the angry look on Thor's face, he fell on the ground. Everyone asked for mercy, offering him whatever they had.

As soon as Thor saw their terror, the fury left him. He calmed down and, as compensation, took the farmer's children with him. That was how Þjálfi and Rǫskva became his servants and have followed him ever since.

Leaving the goats at the farmer's house, Thor and Loki set off for the east. Þjálfi turned out to be a very quick young man, and the haversack was given to him, although there were few provisions inside. Rǫskva went with them.

After crossing the sea, Thor and his companions landed in the Jotunheim. They walked all day through a large forest.

When it was dark, the four sought shelter for the night and arrived at a strange refuge. It was a rather large building, with an entire side occupied by a door. They entered and settled for the night.

Around midnight, the earth was shaken by a great earthquake and the whole house shook. Thor jumped to his feet and called his companions. They advanced through the dark and found a side room. Loki and the others took refuge there, terrified, while Thor stood in the doorway, the hammer in his hand. They heard a groan, then a new noise. Thor went out and, not far away, in the forest, found an individual of enormous size. It was he who had caused the noise that Thor had heard during the night. Enraged at once, Thor girded his Meginjandar belt. However, in the meantime, the other woke up and stood. He towered over Thor with such a stature that, for the first time, Thor lacked the courage to strike with the hammer. Thor asked him who he was.

"My name is Skrýmir," was the answer. "But I don't need to ask for yours. I know you're Thor. Why did you take away my glove?"

He reached for the shelter where Thor and his companions had spent the night. It was not a building but Skrýmir's glove. The side room, in which they had taken refuge, was the thumb.

Skrýmir asked Thor if he wanted his company and Thor answered yes. Skrýmir then took his haversack and set about eating breakfast. Thor and his companions gathered nearby. Later, Skrýmir proposed that they share supplies. He gathered everything in his haversack and put it on his shoulder, walking ahead of them.

The cumbersome companion made great strides, with the four struggling to keep up with him. In the evening, Skrýmir found himself a shelter for the night under an immense oak. "I'd like to go to sleep," he explained to Thor. "But you don't pay compliments. Take the haversack and prepare dinner." Immediately, he closed his eyes. Then Skrýmir fell asleep and began to snore loudly.

Thor took the haversack and started to open it but, unbelievable as it may seem, he was unable to loosen the knots in any way, nor to loosen the strings. When he realized that his efforts were useless, he became furious. He grabbed Mjǫllnir with both hands, strode towards Skrýmir, and hammered him on the head.

Skrýmir woke up. "A little leaf must have fallen on my head," he said. Then he asked Thor, "And you, did you eat? I think you should go and rest now."

Thor replied that they were just going to sleep. He retreated with his companions under another oak, and they could hardly close their eyes in fear.

At midnight, Skrýmir was sleepy and snoring loud enough to make the whole forest resound. Thor approached him, lifted the hammer, and threw it hard at the very center of his skull. He saw it sink deeply into Skrýmir's head.

He woke up and asked, "What is it now?" Did I get an acorn on my head? What happened to you, Thor?"

Thor mumbled that he had just woken up; he said it was midnight and it was time to sleep. He backed away quickly, thinking to himself that if he could have thrown Skrirmir a third blow, he would never have risen again. He sat down, careful to ensure that Skrýmir resumed a deep sleep.

Before the day arrived, Thor realized that Skrýmir had fallen asleep. He jumped on him and, rolling the hammer, cut it down on his temple. This time, Mjǫllnir sank to the handle. However, Skrýmir opened his eyes and rubbed his cheeks, asking. "Has a bird perched on the tree? It seemed to me, as I woke up, that a twig fell on my head. Are you awake too, Thor? Come on, it's time to get up and get dressed. Not much is left to get to Utgard."

Skrýmir stood up and pointed ahead.

"Now I'm going north, to the mountains that you can see over there. You, I guess, are headed east. I heard you say among yourselves that I'm not what they call a small man. Well, if you get to Utgard, you will find people much bigger than me! I imagine it would be better for you to go back but, if you really insist on continuing your journey, I advise you to not make booze in the fortress of Útgarðaloki. His hirðmenn don't tolerate little children like you."

Skrýmir took the haversack, threw it on his back, and walked away through the forest. Thor and his companions did not wish him good luck.

After setting out again at midday, Thor and Loki, along with Þjálfi and Rǫskva, saw a fortress in the middle of a plain. It was so imposing that they had to arch their necks up to their backs before they could see the top.

The doors of Utgard were closed by a gate so powerful that Thor could not open it in any way. Determined to penetrate the fortress, the four crawled between the bars and were able to pass. The doors of the main building were open. They entered and found themselves in a vast hall.

Along two benches sat men of truly gigantic proportions. The four came before the king of the fortress, Útgarðaloki, and greeted him. He turned his gaze slowly to them, grinned, showed his teeth, and said:

"It is too late to ask anyone who has come a long way. But am I wrong or is this young man Thor? I hope you are better than you seem. For which test do you think your companions are ready? Those who do not know an art of some kind or who are better than men will not remain among us.

The last of the group spoke. Loki said, "I have a skill that I am willing to test. There is no one in this room who can eat faster than I can."

Útgarðaloki replied, "It is a skill only if you can prove it."

From the other end of the bench, he called a man. named Logi. to advance into the room and measure himself against Loki.

A trough was placed on the floor of the hall and filled with meat. Loki sat at one end and Logi at the other. Each one ate as fast as he could and they met in the middle. But while Loki had eaten all the meat to the bone, Logi had also eaten the bones and even the trough. It therefore seemed to everyone that Loki had lost the challenge.

Then Útgarðaloki asked what Þjálfi could do. The young man declared that he would compete in a race with whomever Útgarðaloki had chosen.

Útgarðaloki evaluated the young man with a glance and approved the idea. He got up and left the fortress. Outside there was a long plain, the ideal place for the competition to take place. Útgarðaloki called a young man named Hugi and asked him to compete against Þjálfi.

They left and Hugi, who had reached the finish line first, turned to wait for Þjálfi.

"It will be necessary, Þjálfi, for you make the most effort if you want to win the race," urged Útgarðaloki. "But we must admit that nobody came here who could run faster than you."

They had another race and when Hugi reached the finish line, Þjálfi was still as far away as a long arrow shot.

"Although Þjálfi ran well, I don't think he won the race," Útgarðaloki observed. "But we will decide this after running the third lap."

They started again but when Hugi reached the finish line, Þjálfi was not yet halfway through. Everyone declared that the race had its outcome.

At this point, Útgarðaloki turned to Thor. "Men have said great things about your strength and power. In which trials do you want to measure yourself?"

"I could challenge anyone to a drinking contest!" replied Thor

They returned to the hall. Útgarðaloki called his cupbearer and ordered him to take the vítishorn from which he usually drank his hirðmenn. The butler returned immediately with the horn and gave it to Thor.

Útgarðaloki then said, "Emptying this horn in one gulp is what we call a good drink. Some people need two sips but no drinker is so poor as to dry them in three."

Thor examined the horn. It did not have a wide mouth but was rather long. The áss, however, was very thirsty, and so he grabbed the horn and began to gulp it down with great enthusiasm, sure of being able to empty it with a single drink. When his breath failed him, he lowered the horn and examined its level. He had dropped very little.

"A good drink but certainly not substantial," said Útgarðaloki, disappointed. "I never thought that Thor was such a poor drinker, even if they had told me. However, I am sure you will want to empty the horn with a second drink."

Thor did not answer. He brought the horn to his mouth, determined to swallow an abundant gulp. And so he did but no matter how much he tipped his head back, the tip of the horn never rose enough. Thor tried to drink until he was out of breath. When he finally pulled the horn from his lips and looked inside, it seemed to him that the liquid had dropped even less than the first time.

"What is it now, Thor?" Útgarðaloki laughed. "Are you saving yourself for the final drink? If you drink a third sip, I believe you will agree that it will have to be the deepest. We will never call you a worthy man, as the Æsir believe you, if in your other deeds you give no better proof of yourself than you do here."

"I would have found it strange, when I was at home with the Æsir, if such drinks were considered small!" declared Thor. Furious now, he brought the horn to his mouth and drank as much as he could, supporting the drink for a very long time. When he finally looked into the horn, Thor saw that at least the level had dropped significantly.

Útgarðaloki commented, "It is obvious, Thor, that your strength is not as great as we thought. Do you want to face some other tests? It seems to me, though, that you won't look better."

"I can face the toughest challenges!" declared Thor.

"One thing that young people do here and that will seem very little is to lift my cat off the ground. I would certainly not have proposed a similar game to Thor if I had not realized how little you are worth."

A large gray cat leaped into the middle of the room. Thor went up to him, put his hand under his belly, and held him up. But as Thor raised his hand, the cat arched its back. When Thor had raised his arm as high as he could, the cat had raised only one paw from the ground. Thor failed to achieve greater success in this test.

“And this test went as I had planned, ”Útgarðaloki sighed. “The cat is quite large and Thor is weak and small compared to the great men who are here with us.”

Thor was furious. “No matter how small you consider me, someone come forward and fight with me!”

Útgarðaloki looked between the benches and shook his head. “I don't see anyone who can't hold a fight with you as a little thing. But let's see ... there's Elli, my old midwife. Send her to call. She has cut down men who were certainly not weaker than Thor.”

An old woman entered the hǫll and Útgarðaloki told her that she had to fight with Thor. The two grabbed each other, trying to spill onto the ground, but the more strength Thor used, the more Elli resisted. Then the old woman reacted. Thor lost her balance and the fight turned violent. It wasn’t long before Thor collapsed on one knee.

Útgarðaloki then put an end to the clash and said that Thor would no longer have to force himself to fight against others of his hirðmenn.

When night came, Útgarðaloki offered Thor and his companions a place to sleep. The four spent the night at Utgard. None of them felt calm and satisfied.

The next morning, as dawn arrived, Thor stood up with his companions, dressed and got ready to leave. Then came Útgarðaloki, who had a table set for them. Good hospitality, food, and drinks were not lacking. When the four had eaten, they set off.

Útgarðaloki accompanied them for a stretch of road. When they parted, he asked Thor how he thought his journey had gone. Thor admitted the setback immediately. “I know you will say that I am a poor man and I regret it.”

“Now that you have left the fortress, I can tell you the truth,” Útgarðaloki murmured. “And I hope, if I live and continue to reign, that you will never come back to us. In my faith, I would never have let you in, if only I had known how much strength you were gifted and what great danger it represents.

"Know that I have deceived you with a deceptive vision, the sjónhverfingar, since the first meeting in the forest, when I came to receive you, in the disguise of Skrýmir. If you could not open the haversack, it was because I had tied it with an enchanted wire. Then you hit me three times with your Mjölnir and the first one, the weakest, was so powerful that it could have killed me if only it had made a mark. When you saw a mountain near my hǫll with three square valleys at the top, well, those were the marks of your hammer. I used that mountain to ward off your blows, though you didn't notice.

"So it was also for the tests that you and your companions supported against my hirðmenn. The first to compete was Loki. He was very hungry and ate voraciously his part but his adversary, Logi, was the wildfire, and along with the flesh he also burned the bones and the trough.

"When Þjálfi competed with Hugi, well, that was my thought, and we certainly couldn't expect Þjálfi to measure himself fast against it.

"When then you drank from the horn and you seemed to progress slowly, in my faith, it was a prodigy to which I hope I no longer have to attend. The end of the horn reached the ocean, though you didn't notice. When you get to the sea, you can see how much you've lowered it by drinking it."

Útgarðaloki continued: "Nor did it seem to me less astonishing when you tried to lift the cat, and, indeed, I tell you that everyone was terrified when you made him take a paw off the ground. That cat was not what it appeared. It was Jormungandr, the Miðgarðsormr, the serpent that surrounds the whole world. Well, you stretched your arm so hard to lift it almost to the sky.

"And the fight that you sustained so long with my midwife was a great miracle, without giving in except with one knee. Because no one has ever succeeded and will never succeed in not collapsing when Elli, the old age, comes if he becomes old enough to meet her."

And having made this revelation, Útgarðaloki took his leave. "But now we have to separate and it would be better if you didn't come looking for me yet. Next time, I will defend my fortress with even better spells, so that you cannot have power over me."

Upon hearing these words, Thor grabbed the hammer and lifted it into the air, ready to hurl it. However, Útgarðaloki had disappeared before his eyes. Thor returned to the fortress, determined to tear it to pieces, but instead saw only a vast plain, completely empty. Then he turned around and returned to Þrúðvangar.

It is said, however, that after this experience, Thor pondered in his heart to face the Miðgarðsormr, and so it happened later.

Thor Against the Giant Geirrøðr

Once, Loki, who enjoyed flying on the Jotunheim with Frigg's hawk dress, landed in Geirrøðargarðar, the fortresses where jǫtunn Geirrøðr was staying. He went down on a skylight to spy on what was happening inside the hall. Geirrøðr saw this and ordered one of his servants to capture the bird of prey and bring it to him. But the skylight was placed very high on the roof of and the appointee struggled to get up there. Loki had a great time seeing the efforts the man made to reach him and decided, maliciously, to not fly away until the last moment, when the man had finished the dangerous climb.

When the man was about to reach him, Loki spread his wings and waved them vigorously. Then he realized that he had been grabbed by the legs. Loki was thus captured and brought before Geirrøðr. He stared the hawk in the eye and suspected that it was a magically transformed being. He ordered the hawk to reveal himself but Loki fell silent.

Then Geirrøðr locked Loki in a box, letting him go hungry for three long months. When he then pulled out Loki and commanded him once again to speak, Loki certainly did not allow himself to pray. He revealed his identity and, in exchange for his life, promised Geirrøðr that he would make Thor come to Geirrøðargarðr unarmed, without the hammer Mjǫllnir and the megingjarðar belt.

Loki did not have to expend much effort to induce Thor to go to Jotunheim to crush Geirrøðr. The God of Thunder was always well disposed when it came to fighting the odious jotnar. However, we do not know how Loki was able to convince Thor to undertake such a risky expedition, leaving behind his favorite weapon, the hammer Mjǫllnir, and the megingjarðar, the magical belt that multiplied his strength.

After setting off, Thor and his companion spent the night in the home of the giantess Gríðr. A lover of Oðinn, she was the mother of Vidarr the silent.

Knowing the purpose of the journey, Gríðr did not hide from Thor all her knowledge of Geirrøðr. She told him that Geirrøðr was wise, twisted, and difficult to deal with. And because the God of Thunder was unarmed, she lent him her belt of power and the iron gloves she possessed. And with them, she also gave him his rod, the Gríðarvǫlr.

Having left the home of Gríðr, Thor reached the edge of the icy and rushing waters of the Vimur river. This was the largest of all waterways, perhaps one of the Élivágar, perhaps even a stretch of the cosmic ocean. Thor entered the water and waded forward with his companion. Some say it was Loki, clinging to the megingjarðar belt. Others claim it was Þjálfi, tightened to the strap of Thor's shield.

Icy and violent waves ran to meet the God of Thunder as the rocks gave way under his footsteps. While propping himself up with Gríðarvǫlr, Thor advanced furiously against the impetuous currents of the Vimur. When he arrived in the middle of the current, the volume of water had swelled to such an extent that the waves crashed at his shoulders.

Then Thor looked up at the steep rocks and saw Gjálp, Geirrøðr's daughter, astride the two banks of the Vimur river. It was she who urinated and made the river swell. Thor took a large stone from the river and, throwing it at the gýgr, said, "A river must be dammed up at the spring!" He didn't miss the target.

When he reached the bank, Thor clung to a wild rowan tree and pulled himself out of the water. This is why wild rowan is known as "Help of Thor."

Overcoming the flow of stormy waters, Thor thus arrived in Jotunheim, with Þjálfi holding firmly to his belt.

The hearts of the two heroes did not tremble when they found a host of giants waiting for them.

The jotnar stirred up a noise of swords and shields against them. But soon Thor brought them down and put them to flight, forcing them to retreat to their abodes. The God of Thunder could, thus, reach the home of Geirrøðr.

When Thor and Þjálfi came to the Geirrøðargarðar and entered the hǫll, proud and filled with warrior spirit, there was a great commotion among the jotnar. However, the giants took heart and led the God of Thunder, reluctant to make peace, into the lodging they had prepared for him: the stable for goats.

There was only one chair here and Thor sat down. Then, suddenly, the chair rose to the ceiling. Hidden beneath it were Gjálp and Greip, Geirrøðr's daughters, who had decided to break the skull of the God against the roof boards. But Thor, pointing the Gríðarvǫlr rod against the ceiling, pushed the chair back down. There was a great din, followed by a violent shout. Crushed under the chair, Gjálp and Greip had their backbones broken.

Then Geirrøðr invited Thor to hǫll, asking him if he wanted to play with him. There were large hearths all along the walls of the hall. When Thor was in front of the landlord, Geirrøðr pushed the pincers into the fire, took out a piece of incandescent metal, and gave it to him with deadly force. Thor caught it on the fly with his iron gloves (others say he did it with his bare hands) and sent it back to the sender.

Quickly, Geirrøðr dived behind a column. However, the incandescent metal pierced the giant's column and abdomen, then continued its trajectory, broke through a wall, and, falling to the outside of the building, stuck in the ground.

Furious, the jotnar rose in arms. Thor massacred them all, nor did he lack the support of Þjálfi. Thus, Thor defeated Geirrøðr and his unpleasant drinking companions.

Thor Goes Fishing with Hymir

Once, returning from a hunt, the Æsir sat at a banquet, wondering where to find a sufficient amount of beer to accompany lunch. Only with the Ægir could be found cauldrons filled in sufficient quantity to quench their thirst.

So Thor left and found Ægir seated, happy as a child, before his home. "For the Æsir, you will prepare the sweet drink."

The brawler's tone irritated Ægir, who immediately thought of how to turn the request against the Gods.

"If all of you want me to make it, then give me a suitable pot."

The request inflicted difficulty upon the Æsir, who, despite searches, were unable to find a pot large enough to supply all the Gods with beer. Then Týr approached Thor and confidently told him, "The abode, to the east of the Élivágar, on the edge of the sky, of the wise Hymir. He is my irascible parent and has a very large boiler."

"But will we get that container to put on the fire?"

"Only if we act with cunning and deception, my friend," was Týr's reply.

Leaving Asgard, Týr and Thor traveled throughout the day amid the rumble of the wagon wheels until they came to the house of Egill, a giant of the stony ground, to whom Thor left his great-horned goats for safekeeping. Then, the two continued on their way until, having reached the limit of the sky, they arrived at the hǫll of Hymir.

The welcome that Týr received was certainly not enthusiastic. On one side was the hateful grandmother, who had nine hundred heads. The mother—all adorned with gold, with white eyebrows—came forward, holding out a glass of beer to her son.

Then Hymir burst into the house. Deformed of appearance, despicable, with a frozen beard, he advanced into the hǫll, rattling the icicles.

"Hi, Hymir! Look, our son has come, whom we have been waiting for after a long journey. He is accompanied by the opponent of HrOdr, the friend of men, who is called Thor. Here they are sheltered, at the bottom of the hill, behind the column...

Immediately, the column shattered under Hymir's gaze; the main beam broke in two, dropping the eight pots hanging over the head of the two Æsir. Only one, well-shaped, remained intact. Týr and Thor came forward. Hymir stared at Thor with a suspicious look. Nothing good was presented to him at the sight of the áss, well known for moving the women of the jotnars to tears.

Immediately, three bulls were led from the herd. Hymir ordered them to be cooked. The animals were beheaded and cooked. The dinner was set and Thor alone ate two bulls.

Hrungnir's gray confidences seemed to Hymir, the portion of Thor being a bit abundant. "If you're going to have dinner tomorrow night," he said to his guests, "the three of us should get some food by hunting or fishing."

When it was day, Hymir got up, dressed, and got ready to go fishing in the boat. Thor jumped to his feet, quickly ready, and asked Hymir to take him with him to the sea. Hymir replied that he would be of little help. "You will freeze if I stay away from you, as it is my intention."

For this, Thor wanted to hit him with the hammer. He stayed, however, because he intended to prove his strength elsewhere. "I will row for so long and so far from the shore that you will be the first to go back," he warned. "Rather, give me bait for fishing."

"Turn to the herds if you have the hugr, you, the massacre of the Danirs of the mountains!" mocked Hymir. "I guess it's easy for you to get bait from a bull!"

Thor went to the forest, where he had seen Hymir's cattle. A black bull came forward. It was Himinhrjótr, the largest and most magnificent beast in the whole herd. Thor removed his head and took it with him to the coast.

Hymir had already pushed the ship into the water. Thor climbed aboard, sat aft, grabbed the oars, and began to row. At the bow, Hymir had to admit that Thor's rowing produced good speed. The jǫtunn began to row in turn, and for a while, the ship proceeded over the dark waters of the úthaf.

At one point, Hymir said they could now stop to catch sole but Thor retorted that he intended to go a little further out and made another effort. "It would be dangerous to go any farther," said Hymir. "We could meet Jormungandr."

"To tell the truth, I'd like to go a little farther," Thor replied, and proceeded. Hymir began to feel rather upset."

Then Thor pulled the oars into the boat and the two set to fish. Hymir threw the hook and, out of grumpiness, fished two whales. Meanwhile, at the stern, Thor prepared a very strong fishing line, with a sturdy hook. He hooked the head of the ox and threw it overboard.

The bait came to the bottom. Jormungandr swallowed the head of the ox but the hook stuck in his jaws. When the snake noticed it, he pulled so hard that both of Thor's fists bumped against the nǫkkvi's frisata. Furious, Thor, heard his ásmegin grow. He planted his feet on the bottom of the boat and pulled up the snake. Some say, certainly exaggerating, that Thor had even broken through the keel and that his feet were planted on the bottom of the úthaf. Jormungandr's head emerged from the water and struck the side of the nǫkkvi, spilling high waves into the fragile boat. It may well be said that he never witnessed terrible scenes who did not see this with his own eyes. Thor looked at the snake, which, in turn, stared at him from below, dripping poison. Then Thor brandished the Mjǫllnir and hurled it at the serpent's head. The whole earth shook and the steep rocks groaned among the wolf howls.

They say that, when he saw Jormungandr, Hymir became livid with terror. He grabbed the fishing knife and cut the line so that the snake could sink back into the abyss. Infuriated, Thor gave Hymir a violent punch behind the ear, knocking him headlong out of the boat. After that, because the keel of the boat was now broken, Thor forded the uthaf until it reached the mainland.

When they returned to shore, Hymir stared at Thor. "It was established that we would each do half the work. So, choose: Either take the two whales to the farm, or moor the ship."

Thor, without a word, grabbed the ship by the bow and lifted it, with the two whales and the oars. Holding it high above his head, he crossed the hollow under the cliff, until he reached the fortress of Hymir.

Thor's showdown was not enough to lift Hymir out of his irritation. During dinner, the jǫtunn did not stop provoking him. "A man cannot be defined as 'strong' only because he is vigorous. 'Strong' is only the one who will succeed in breaking my cup!

This was a glass goblet, apparently fragile but actually very robust. As soon as he had it in his hands, Thor threw it at a stone column. The pillar fell apart but the chalice was brought back intact to Hymir.

So, the lord of the goats stood up, appealing to all his ásmegin. An instant later, the cup fell to pieces against Hymir's skull.

"I have lost a piece of great value, now that the chalice has been torn from my knees," grumbled the junnt. "How sad, never to say, never again. Beer, here you are! But there is still a test to be overcome." He angrily raised his gaze on his two guests. "If you can get my cauldron out of here."

Immediately, Týr tried to lift the huge pot. Twice he tried but he couldn't even move it. Thor grabbed him by the edge and tipped him over his head. It was so heavy that the Thunder God's feet sank into the floor. Then Thor moved towards the exit of the hǫll.

The two fugitives, who had to turn back, had not traveled far, however. Behind them, towards the east, ranks with many heads advanced in arms. Hymir, infuriated, guided them.

Thor took the cauldron off his shoulders, laid it down on a song, and, feeling a sudden desire for slaughter, wielded Mjǫllnir. All the jotnar struck death.

Full of vigor, Thor reached the Æsir þing, carrying the large cauldron that had been Hymir's. Thanks to it, from that day on, all the Æsir could drink to satiety.

Thor vs. Hrungnir

It is said that, once, while Thor was in the east fighting the trǫlls, Odin rode on Sleipnir's back in Jotunheim.

Thus, he arrived at the jǫtunn named Hrungnir. He judged the horse that galloped both in the air and in the water to be extraordinary and asked for the identity of the man with the golden helmet, who was riding him. In response, and without revealing himself, Odin said he was ready to bet his head that in all of Jotunheim there was not a horse equal to his.

"Yours is really a good horse," conceded Hrungnir, "but I have one that has much longer leaps, and is called Gullfaxi ['golden mane']."

He jumped on Gullfaxi and galloped after Oðinn, determined to make him take back his superb words. But Odin rode so fast that, in an instant, he disappeared over a hill. Hrunginr was so taken with the fury of the chase that he did not notice that he had passed the gates of Ásgrindr and was now in Asgard, in the Æsir fortress.

When Hrungnir came to the gates of Valhalla, the Æsir invited him to drink. They were then brought the huge jugs from which usually drank Thor. Hrungnir drank them all.

When the jǫtunn was drunk, he did not stop the boastings. He said that he would lift Valhalla and take it to Jotunheim, and that he would have collapsed Asgard, killed all the Gods, and brought Freyja and Sif with him to his home.

While Freyja poured him a drink, he swore that he would drink all the Æsir's beer.

Very soon, the Æsir grew tired of the bluster of Hrungnir and invoked Thor. The God immediately appeared in the hǫll, wielding the hammer Mjǫllnir. He looked around furiously and asked, "Who allowed the jntars from the twisted mind to drink in Valhalla? And why is Freyja mixing beer in Hrungnir, as if she were at an Æsir banquet?"

Hrungnir stared at Thor with eyes that were anything but friendly. "It was Odin who invited me to drink, and I'm under his protection."

"It's an invitation you'll regret before leaving!" replied Thor.

"You will certainly not accomplish a memorable task, and you will be branded cowardly if you kill me while I am unarmed," Hrungnir said. "It was really silly for me to have left my shield and my hen at home. If I had my weapons here, we could fight. I think it would be a more valuable test if you fought with me on the borders of the Grjótúngarðar."

Having said that, Hrungnir returned to the Jotunheim, galloping impetuously.

The hasty departure of Hrungnir from Asgard left Thor furious. The jntar had offended him personally, threatening to kidnap his wife, Sif. What's more, according to what some warmers claim, it seems that Hrungnir had taken Þrúðr, the daughter of Thor.

The fury was also joined with a singular excitement. It was the first time that Thor had been challenged to a duel. He, therefore, had every reason to hurry to the Grjótúngarðar and to make Hrungnir eat his bluster.

Among the jotnar, there was much talk of Hrungnir's journey to Asgard and, above all, of the fact that he had decided to clash with Thor.

To the inhabitants of Jotunheim did not escape the fact that the duel between the two maximum champions would have some important consequences in terms of who won. They were certain that they would suffer great evils if Thor killed Hrungnir, as he was the strongest of them all. Thus it was that the jotnar shaped a clay man and placed him at the borders of the Grjótúngarðar. It was called Mǫkkurkálfi. They didn't find a heart big enough for it until they tore one from a mare, and it still wasn't firmly attached when Thor arrived.

As for Hrungnir, he stood beside the clay man, waiting for his adversary. His heart, as is known, was made of hard stone and equipped with three sharp horn tips, from which the symbol called Hrungnishjartr originates. His head was also stone, as was his broad and thick shield, which he held in front of him while he waited for Thor on the borders of the Grjótúnagarðar. As a weapon, he had a whetstone, a huge sharpening stone. He held it over his shoulder and was certainly not reassuring to see.

Thor left no time in between, such was his desire to fight with Hrungnir. He jumped on his chariot. Þjálfi was with him. His arrival did not go unnoticed. Even the Ginnungagap trembled when Thor left Asgard. The firmament caught fire, reverberating with thunder, lashed by hail as it descended to earth. After that, the mountains broke apart and the land itself was about to break open when Thor entered Jotunheim, without consideration, on his chariot pulled by the goats.

Hrungnir immediately put himself on the defensive

Þjálfi ran to Hrungnir and said, "You are not safe, jǫtunn, if you hold the shield in front. Know that Thor saw you. It will go underground and hit you from below."

Faster than his hand than with his brain, Hrungnir put the clear shield under his feet and remained motionless, lifting the whetstone with two hands. Soon after, between lightning and thunder, he saw Thor advancing. Thor whirled Mjölnir and hurled it from afar at Hrungnir. Hrungnir raised the whetstone and pulled it against him. The hammer intercepted the whetstone in the middle of the trajectory and shattered it. The fragments scattered on the earth and from them originated the stones from which men draw their whorls. However, a very hard flint struck Thor in the forehead and he fell to the ground.

The Mjölnir hit Hrungnir's head in full, smashing his skull into a thousand pieces. The junnt collapsed on Thor and a foot fell across his neck.

Meanwhile, the Mǫkkurkálfi, struck by Þjálfi, fell with little dignity.

Immediately, Þjálfi went to Thor to remove Hrungnir's foot from him but he did not have enough strength. All the Æsir came and tried to free him but none succeeded.

Then little Magni, son of Thor and Járnsaxa, came forward. Despite his age, he lifted Hrungnir's foot effortlessly and freed Thor.

Thor stood up, welcoming his son. "You will certainly become very powerful," he said, pleased. "Here, I give you the horse Gullfaxi, which before had belonged to Hrungnir."

Then Thor returned to his home but he always had the fragments stuck in his head. Then came a sorceress named Gróa, wife of Aurvandill the Brave. She cast a spell for him and the whetstone began to stir. When Thor noticed that he could be freed from the hedge, he wanted to reward Gróa. To make her happy, he told her about a time when he had forded the Elivágar from north to south, taking Aurvandill out of Jötunheimr. As proof of this, he said that an Aurvandill's big toe was sticking out of the basket and frozen, so that he had broken it and thrown it into the sky. "You can see it. It is the star called Aurvandilstá." He added that Aurvandill would be home soon. Gróa was so happy that she forgot the spell, and the whetstone remained stuck in Thor's head.

That's why you don't have to throw a whetstone through a room. Each time a whetstone falls to the ground, the fragment is shaken inside Thor's head, causing him great pain.

Thor, the Stolen Hammer, and Freyja's Unexpected Wedding

One night, while he was sleeping, Thor was robbed of his precious hammer. The thief was a giant named Þrymr. On awakening, and upon realizing the theft, the God was shaken by anger and tormented by worry. He then confided in Loki, who, due to his intelligence and cunning, was the only one able to help him. Loki did not waste time. With Thor, he went to Freyja to borrow her hawk disguise. The Goddess willingly gave it to him. Loki flew past the Æsir enclosure until he reached Jötunheimr. Þrymr sat on a small hill, combed the hair of his horses, and wrapped a gold collar for the dogs. He asked Loki, "Whatever happened among the Æsir and among the elves that you come to Jötunheimr?"

"There is trouble among the Æsir, trouble among the elves," replied Loki. "Are you the one who hid Thor's hammer?"

Mrymr replied that, yes, it was him. He had stolen the precious hammer. "I concealed it," he said, "eight miles under the earth. No one can get it back unless you bring me Freyja in marriage."

So, Loki flew and returned to the Æsir precinct. Thor met him anxiously and invited him, before sitting down, to report the results of the mission. So went Thor and Loki from the Goddess Freyja and proposed her to be the bride of the giant. Freyja mounted on all fury and became terribly angry—so much so that all the mansions of the Gods were shaken. Even the precious Brísingamen necklace shot away from her chest. She said, "Do you really think he has such a wild desire for males to go with you to Jötunheimr?"

The Gods gathered at council. Now they absolutely had to find a way to recover Thor's precious hammer. The best suggestion came from Heimdallr, God of the very bright Æsir, who nevertheless knew the future as the Vanir. Heimdallr said, "Let us adorn Thor with the wedding garment, let us put the Brísingamen necklace on his neck! We will hang a bunch of keys by his side and make a woman's dress cover his knees! Then we will simulate the chest with big stones and we will adjust the hair well."

This suggestion pleased Thor very little. "The Gods will give me an invert," he said, "if I let myself be dressed as a bride."

Loki replied: "Soon the giants will live in Ásgarðr if you don't recover the hammer!"

This remark eliminated any hesitation.

Thor was therefore adorned with wedding garments and wore the Brísingamen necklace from Freyja around his neck. A bunch of keys hung from his side and a woman's robe covered his knees. Then his chest was simulated with large stones and his hair was well arranged. When this was done, Loki said, "I will be your maid and I will take you to Jötunheimr."

So Loki and Thor departed on the chariot of the God pulled by goats. They ran so fast that the mountains fell to pieces and the earth burned in flames.

Þrymr, lord of the giants, was preparing to welcome the bride. He said. "Soon, prepare the benches to receive Freyja, daughter of Njörðr! I have cows and oxen with golden horns and I have many jewels, necklaces, and treasures but I miss her alone."

In the evening, a grand banquet was prepared and the giants were served beer. Thor was very hungry and ate greedily. Alone, he devoured an ox and eight salmon, delicious morsels destined for women. He also drank three barrels of mead. Þrymr was surprised and suspicious; therefore, he said, "Have you ever seen a bride eat so greedily and a woman drink so much mead?"

The very skillful and astute little maid who was sitting in front hastened to explain: "Freyja had not touched food for eight days, so much was her desire to come to Jötunheimr."

Þrymr seemed convinced; again, however, he marveled and became suspicious when he bent over the bride to kiss her. The look was so fiery that he jumped back into the banquet hall. Then he asked, "Why are Freyja's eyes so terrible? It seems that there is a fire in them."

The very skillful and astute maid who was sitting in front of her hastened to explain: "Freyja hasn't closed her eyes for eight nights, so much was her desire to come to Jötunheimr."

At that moment, the giant's sister entered the room and wanted to ask for a wedding gift. She said to Thor, "Take the gold rings out of your hands if you want to win my goodwill and my love!"

Then spoke Þrymr, lord of the giants: "Bring the hammer to consecrate the bride. Place Mjölnir on her lap and consecrate us together by the hand of Vár!"

Thor, in the depths of his heart, recognized the hammer. He immediately grabbed it and, first, hit Þrymr to death with it and then, immediately after, all his own. Nor did he spare the life of the giant's sister. She who had dared to ask for the wedding gifts received a hammering instead of gold, a loud barrel instead of rings. So the son of Odin recovered the precious hammer.

How Freyr Lost His Sword

There was a man named Gymir who had a wife named Aurboða. She was of the line of the mountain giants. Their daughter was Gerðr, the most beautiful of all women.

One day, Freyr looked at all the worlds on Odin's throne. When he turned towards the north, he saw, on a farm, a large and beautiful building. Towards this house, a woman went. When she raised her hands and opened the door before her, light spread in her air and over the sea and all the worlds lit up.

Thus, Freyr was punished for his audacity in sitting on that sacred seat reserved only for Odin. He went away full of pain. When he returned home, he neither spoke nor slept nor drank, and no one dared speak to him.

Then Njörðr called Skyrnir, Freyr's messenger, and ordered him to go to Freyr, to talk to him and ask him why he was so angry he wouldn't talk to anyone. Skírnir said that he was ready to go, though reluctantly, and stated that bad answers should be expected.

When he got to Freyr, Skyrnir asked him why he was so sad and wouldn't talk to anyone. Freyr said that he had seen a beautiful woman and that he was distressed and would not live long if he could not have her.

"And now you have to leave and ask for her hand for me. For this, I will reward you well."

Skírnir replied by saying that he would carry out the embassy but that Freyr had to give him his sword. Freyr did not pray and gave him the sword.

When he arrived at the house of the woman, Skírnir found some biting dogs bound together at the entrance, preventing him from passing. He then turned to a shepherd who was sitting on a hill and asked him in which way the house could be accessed.

"Are you dying or already dead?" the pastor asked him in reply. "No one comes out of that house alive!"

However, Skírnir did not allow himself to be impressed by his words. Again, he returned to the house. And, again, the dogs at the door barked until, hearing this noise, the beautiful Gerðr sent a servant to see what was happening.

"There is a man who has dismounted," said the servant, "and makes his steed graze in front of the house."

Gerðr told her to let him in and offer him a drink.

"I have here with me," said Skírnir, "eleven golden apples. I will give them to you, in exchange for your love, as long as you say that Freyr is, for you, the dearest of all living beings. "

Gerðr refused the apples and, with them, the love of the God. "Tell Freyr that I will never live with him," she replied coldly.

Skírnir then tried to offer her the Draupnir ring, the magical talisman that Odin had placed at the stake of Baldr. "From this ring," he said, "every nine nights, another eight of equal weight come out."

Gerðr also refused the ring. "In the precincts of my father," she said, "certainly gold is not lacking."

To overcome her obstinacy, Skírnir decided to let go of the gifts and flattery and to proceed to the threats. He drew the sword that had been a gift from Freyr and, showing it to the maiden, said that he would cut off her head if she did not consent. And because Gerðr still insisted on her refusal, Skírnir threatened to kill her father, the giant Gymir, in order to get her consent.

However, considering that the threats were useless, Skírnir decided to resort to magic: "With the magic wand, I will hit you. I will ask you, young girl, at my command; there you will go where the children of men never again will see you."

He predicted all sorts of punishments. She would live forever with her eyes turned to the kingdom of the dead, she would feed on disgusting food, she would become horrible to the eye, and she would always be locked up in the gates of the beyond, suffering the worst torments and persecutions from demonic beings, forced to lie with the giants and live with the most monstrous of them: the giant with three heads. She would never enjoy the joys of love but would be confined to the realm of the dead, where she would have drunk nothing but goat piss.

It was only before the power of magic that Gerðr finally surrendered. Then she raised her glass, offered to drink to Skírnir, and declared herself willing to give Freyr that "appointment" for which he so longed...

"Long is a night, two are long; how can I languish for three?"

The Death of Baldr

This story begins when Baldr, the good, dreamed big dreams and saw harbingers of danger to his life. When he told the Æsir about these dreams, they gathered to council. It was decided to demand, for Baldr, a guarantee of safety from every kind of damage.

Frigg got oaths that everything would be safe for Baldr: fire and water, iron and every kind of metal, stones, earth, trees, disease, animals, birds, poison, snakes.

And this was done and defined. It was a pastime for Baldr and the Æsir that, while he stood upright, all the others aimed at him, some from far away, some from close by, hitting him, some hurling stones. Whatever was done, nothing hurt, and to all of them it seemed a great advantage.

But when Loki saw this, he was sorry that nothing would harm Baldr. Taking the form of a woman, he went to Frigg. Frigg asked the woman if she knew what the Æsir had done.

Then Frigg said, "Neither weapon nor wood can harm Baldr. I have been sworn in by all things."

Loki then asked, "Have all things sworn to spare Baldr?"

Frigg replied, "A small plant grows to the west of the Valhöll which has the name mistletoe; I thought it was too young to demand an oath."

Immediately afterward, the woman left.

Loki took the mistletoe seedling, tore it up, and went to the Æsir.

There Höðr was alone, outside the circle of others, for he was blind.

Loki said to him, "Why don't you throw something on Baldr?"

He replied, "Because I don't see where Baldr is and also because I am without weapons."

Loki said, "Do as others do. Honor Baldr. I will show you where he is. Hit him with this stick."

Höðr took the mistletoe and threw it at Baldr according to Loki's directions. The blow pierced him and knocked him to the ground.

And this has been the greatest misfortune among the Gods and among men.

When Baldr lay dead, all the Gods were voiceless and so the hands stretched to catch him fell back. They looked at each other and everyone had a single thought against the one who had taken that action.

But no one could take revenge, so sacred was that place of peace.

And when the Æsir tried to speak, they were rather crying in the throat, so that no one could express their pain to the others. Odin suffered this evil more than any other because he knew better than anyone what great loss and what damage they were to suffer in Baldr's death.

When the Gods returned to their senses, Frigg spoke and asked who among the Æsir wanted to earn all his love and benevolence, who wanted to walk the road to Hel and see if he could find Baldr and offer Hel a ransom if she had allowed Baldr to go home to Asgard.

Hermóðr the bold, son of Odin, volunteered for this trip. He took Sleipnir, the horse of Odin.

The Æsir took Baldr's body and brought him to the sea.

Hringhorni was called the ship of Baldr. It was the largest of all ships. The Gods wanted to use it to travel to the pyre of Baldr. However, the ship did not move.

Then he was sent to Jötunheimr to call the giantess named Hyrrokkin. She came upon a wolf and had poisonous snakes for bridles. She stepped down from her mount and Odin called four berserkers to guard that mount. They couldn't help but knock it over.

Then Hyrrokkin stood against the bow of the ship and, at the first push, moved it so that the fire came out of the supports and the lands trembled. Then Thor grabbed the hammer and would have smashed her head if the Gods had not interceded to spare her.

Then the body of Baldr was brought to the ship. He saw his wife, Nanna, daughter of Nep. Her heart was broken with grief and she died. Also, she was placed on the pyre, which was set on fire.

Thor was present and consecrated the pyre with Mjölnir. However, a dwarf named Lítr came running to him. Thor gave him a kick and made him end up in the fire, where he burned.

At this cremation ceremony, people of various lineages intervened. Primarily, it was Odin. With him came Frigg and the Valkyries and his ravens. Freyr arrived on the wagon pulled by the boar named Gullinbursti or Slidrugtanni. Heimdallr straddled Gulltoppr while Freyja drove her cats. A great crowd of giants and ursars also came.

Odin placed, at the stake, the gold ring called Draupnir. It was its nature that, on every ninth night, eight gold rings of equal weight detached from it as it dropped.

Baldr's horse was led to the stake with all the harnesses.

Of Hermóðr it is said that he rode nine nights in valleys so dark and deep that he could see nothing before him until he reached the river Gjöll and galloped over the bridge above it. It was covered with shining gold. Móðguðr was the virgin who looked at the bridge. She asked him for her name and her lineage and said that the day before, they had crossed the bridge with five groups of dead men. "But the bridge is not less beneath you alone and then you do not have the color of dead men: Why go the way of Hel, thou?"

He replied, "I will ride to Hel to find Baldr. Did you see Baldr on the way to Hel?"

She said that Baldr had crossed the bridge of Gjöll there, and down the north was the road to Hel.

Then Hermóðr rode until he reached the gates of Hel. There he dismounted, secured the harness, climbed back, and gave a spur. The steed leaped with such impetus over the gates that he certainly did not even touch them.

Then Hermóðr rode to the hall and got off his horse. He entered the hall and saw Baldr, his brother, sitting on the highest seat. Hermóðr spent the night there.

In the morning, Hermóðr asked Hel to tell him that Baldr was going home with him and said how great the pain was among the Æsir.

But Hel replied that this was the occasion on which it would be possible to prove whether Baldr was so universally loved as was said. "If all things in the worlds, living and dead, will mourn him, then he will return to the Æsir. However, he will remain at Hel if someone refuses to do it and doesn't want to cry."

Then Hermóðr got up. Baldr took him out of the room. He took the Draupnir ring and sent it to Odin as a souvenir. Nanna sent Frigg a cloth and other gifts, including a gold ring for Fulla.

Then Hermóðr retraced his steps on horseback and returned to Asgard, where he reported all the facts he had seen and heard.

Immediately the Æsir sent messengers all over the world to ask that Baldr be wept over and, thus, taken away from Hel.

And they all did, men and every other living being, and the earth and the stones and trees and every metal. As you will have seen, these things cry when they come out of the frost and into heat.

When the messengers returned home, having done their job well, they found an old woman sitting in a dwelling. Her name was Þökk.

They also begged her to cry about Baldr to bring him from Hel.

But she said, "Þökk will cry with dry eyes over Baldr's journey to the stake. From the old man's son neither alive nor dead never had the advantage. Keep Hel what he has."

It is supposed that it was Loki, disguised as an old woman, who brought the greatest evil among the Æsir.

After the death of Baldr Æsir was very angry with Loki and wanted to capture him. But Loki escaped from Asgard and hid in a mountain. Here, Loki built a house with four doors so that he could look out in all directions. During the day, Loki would often shapeshift into a salmon and hide in the river.

In the evening, Loki sat near the fire pit inside his house and wondered about the punishment of the Æsir. While he sat there, he entertained himself by making a fishing net with linen yarn.

One day, Loki was looking out from one of his doors when he saw the Æsir coming to him. He quickly jumped up and threw the linen net into the fire, then ran down to the river.

When the Æsir arrived at the house, Kvasir was the first one to enter. Kvasir looked around the house and spotted the remains of the net in the fire. He spoke with the Æsir about his findings and they made a copy of it.

All the Æsir began to drag the net and placed it in the waterfall. However, Loki swam in front, moved down, and hid himself between two stones.

The Æsir believed that someone was hiding there, so they threw and pulled out the net. However, he was not there. Again, they threw it.

Loki, realizing he was near the sea, jumped over the net and swam back into the waterfall.

This time the Æsir saw him and they returned to the waterfall. Thor found himself in the middle of the river and dragged another net towards the sea.

Loki realized that he would have to dive into the sea, though it was dangerous, or jump through the net. He finally decided to throw himself headlong into the net.

Thor grabbed the fish. It almost slipped from his hands but he managed to hold it by the tail.

Loki had been captured and could not hope for mercy.

Now that Loki had been captured by the Æsir, they wanted revenge for the death of Baldr. They dragged Loki to a cave and took three flat stones. They put them on their edges and made a hole through them.

The Æsir caught Loki's sons, Vali and Narfi. They transformed Vali into a wolf, who devoured his own brother. Narfi. The Gods, using magic with Narfi's guts, bound Loki, who was then placed on top of the three stones.

For the last punishment, Skadi took a poisonous snake and placed it near Loki so that its poison dropped to his face. Sigyn, Loki's wife, decided to stay and help Loki by holding a basket on his head to catch the poison of the snake.

Every time the bowl is full, she leaves to empty it. At that moment, the poison drips on Loki's face, making him shake violently in pain so that the whole earth trembles.

How Freyja Obtained Brísingamen

Freyja, daughter of Njörðr, once lived with Odin because she was his beloved. At the palace, four dwarves lived in a stone: Álfrigg, Dvalinn, Berlingr, and Grérr. They were skilled artisans who succeeded in everything that they proposed for tariff. Odin loved Freyja very much, as she was the most attractive woman there was. She owned a beautiful and robust dwelling. It is said that when the doors were locked, no one could enter against her will.

One day, it happened that Freyja went to the stone where the dwarves lived. She found it open and saw that they were finishing a beautiful gold necklace. The Goddess seemed rather beautiful to the dwarves. For this reason, when she asked to buy the necklace in exchange for gold and silver and other precious things, they declared that they did not need wealth but said that everyone had surrendered a part of each of them. To get the necklace, the Goddess had to adhere to their will. When the four nights passed happened from the necklace and returned home. However, she said nothing to anyone and acted as if nothing had happened.

It is said, however, that Loki, who was a courtier of Odin and enjoyed his trust, learned that Freyja possessed the necklace. Moreover, he knew how she had obtained it. He immediately went to Odin and told him everything. Odin ordered him to seize the necklace for him. Loki replied that it was not possible, as no one could enter Freyja's home against her will. Odin, however, insisted. Loki was to go immediately and not come back without the necklace. So Loki went away, complaining.

He then went to the residence of Freyja but found it locked. He tried to penetrate it but in vain. It was cold outside and he was beginning to shiver. Then he turned into a fly and flew around the locks and doors, looking for an opening. Finally, he found a hole on the roof so small that only a needle could pass through it. In that way, he entered the house. When he entered, he paid close attention. They all slept inside. He approached Freyja's bed and saw that she was lying asleep with the necklace around her neck. The clip, however, was located below her neck. Loki turned into a flea and rested on the Goddess's cheek, stinging her. She awoke and turned over in bed, then fell asleep again. Loki took off his disguise, slipped off the necklace, opened the door, and went out to Odin.

The next morning, after awakening, Freyja noticed that the door was open, though not forced, and that her precious necklace had disappeared. She knew what had happened, so as soon as she was dressed, she immediately went to Odin, complaining about his behavior. She also wanted the necklace given back to her. Odin said he would not give it back, due to the way she had come to possess it, except on one condition: Freyja should give birth to enmity between two kings, each of whom had subjugated twenty other sovereigns, so that by magic and curse they were forced to fight and kill each other, then be reborn immediately only to start the fight again. Thus did magic provoke the eternal battle between Högni and Heðinn. Odin then returned the precious jewel to Freyja.

An Otter Ransom and a Cursed Ring

One day, Odin, Loki, and Hoenir were exploring the world and arrived at a river. While walking along the river, they came to a waterfall and saw an otter that was eating a salmon.

Loki threw a stone, hitting the otter in the head and killing it. The Gods picked up the otter and the salmon and continued to walk until they came to Hreidmar, a powerful man who had mastered the arts of magic.

The Æsir asked for a place to sleep for the night and offered to share the otter and the salmon with him.

When Hreidmar saw the dead otter, he called to Fafnir and Regin his two sons. "My sons, those travelers have murdered your brother Otr"(who was able to shapeshift into an otter). So, Fafnir and Regin took the three Æsir prisoner and bound them to a chair, seeking revenge for their brother. The Æsir offered wealth in compensation for their freedom, so Hreidmar ripped off the otter fur and created a bag, then asked them to fill it with red gold. Odin told Loki to travel to Svartalheim and find red gold to pay the debt.

Luckily for Loki, he knew where to find it: precisely, in Svartalheim, from the dwarf Andvari. At the sight of Loki, he shapeshifted himself into a fish and jumped into the river. However, after a while, Loki fished the shifted dwarf.

Loki demanded all the treasure for his life. Because Andvari's life was in the hands of Loki, the dwarf agreed to his demands but tried to hide a gold ring (Andvaranaut) inside his hand. Loki saw him and demanded it, even after Andvari begged Loki, as this magic ring had the power to created more gold for him. Loki refused and Andvari cursed the ring, yelling that it would destroy anyone who possessed it.

Loki, not caring about the warning, went back to the farmhouse and showed Odin the gold. Odin noticed the ring and tried to take it for himself, giving the rest of the gold to Hreidmar. However, Hreidmar started to inspect the bag and noticed that a single whisker was still visible.

Odin admitted that the agreement had not yet been satisfied, so he placed the Andvaranaut over the whisker, covering it completely. Now the debt had been paid. Returning to Asgard, Loki kept thinking about Andvari's curse.

It did not take long for the ring's curse to take hold. Regin and Fafnir soon demanded that Hriedmar share the treasure. When the father refused to give them even a single coin, he was quickly murdered by Fafnir.

The ring also created a wedge between the brothers because, while Hreidmar was on the ground covered in his own blood, Regin asked Fafnir to share the gold equally. Fafnir refused and threatened to give his brother the same fate as their father if he didn't leave the place. Fafnir picked up his father's helmet, Ægis the helm of death, and placed it on his own head.

Fafnir took the treasure and hid himself in the lair Gnita-Heath, where the cursed treasure transformed Fafnir into a dragon.

With no family or money, Regin went on to serve as a royal blacksmith to King Hjalprek in Denmark.

One day there arrived a widowed pregnant woman from the lands of the Volsungs. Soon after, she gave birth to the legendary Sigurd. Regin took him as his foster son. After Sigurd had grown, Regin spoke to him about the dragon, Fafnir, and the great treasure that he was guarding at Gnita-Heath. Using his talents in blacksmithing, Regin forged the sword Gram, made from the shattered pieces of a blade given a long time ago to the Volsung family by Odin himself. This sword was so sharp that Sigurd cut Regin's anvil in two with one blow.

Armed with his sword, Gram, Sigurd traveled to Gnita-Heath, where he waited for Fafnir. When Fafnir came out from his lair, Sigurd surprised him and stabbed the dragon through the belly, killing him.

After the dragon died, Sigurd cut out Fafnir's heart. Upon tasting his blood, he obtained the supernatural power to speak with birds. Sigurd, listening to the warnings of the birds, became suspicious of Regin, who had followed him to Gnita-Heath. He killed Regin and then left the dragon lair.

Sigurd traveled in the mountain of Hindarfjall, surrounded by a wall of flame, until he found a house with a woman inside, equipped with a helmet and a mail coat.

He took out the sword and cut off the mail coat. The woman woke up and presented herself. Her name was Hild but people called her the Valkyrie Brynhild.

Sigurd left the house, mounted his horse again, and arrived at the court of King Gjuki and his wife, Grimhild. Their children were two males (Gunnar and Högni) and two females (Gudrun and Gudny), while Gothormr was considered a stepson

Sigurd stayed with them and married Gudrun, creating a path of brotherhood with the two sons: Gunnar and Hogni.

Because Gunnar was in love with Brynhild, the next day Sigurd and the two brothers traveled to ask him for Brynhild's hand. However, she had sworn to marry only the man who had tried to ride through the flickering flame.

Gunnar tried to ride through those flames but his horse, called Goti, would simply not jump into the fire.

Because Sigurd's Grani horse refused to be ridden by Gunnar, they exchanged their forms and their names. Sigurd jumped on his horse and rode through the flame.

In the evening, Sigurd married Brynhild, drew out his sword Gram, and spent the night with her. In the morning, he gave Brynhild the gold ring Andvarinaut, which he had received from Fafnir. In exchange, he took another ring. The next morning, Brynhild, Sigurd, and Gunnar returned to their same forms and they all returned to King Gjuki. Shortly after, Gunrun gave birth to Sigmund and Svanhild.

One day, Brynhild and Gudrun went to the river to wash their hair. Brynhild walked a little farther along the river and up the mountain because she didn't want to wash in the dirty water touched by Gudrun. She thought her husband was braver than Sigurd. Gudrun reminded her that was Sigurd was the bravest man in the world for killing both Fafnir and Regin and claiming all their treasures.

Brynhild replied that Gunnar had ridden through the flame, while Sigurd would not dare.

Gudrun, laughing, told that was not her husband, reminding her that the ring he gave to her had been taken by the dragon Fafnir.

Brynhild then returned home to Gunnar and tried to convince him and his brother Hogni to kill Sigurd. They and Sigurd were blood brothers, so they couldn't do it but spoke with their brother Gothorm about killing Sigurd. One night, he entered Sigurd's house and pierced him with his sword while Sigurd was sleeping. Sigurd woke up and, with a single blow of his sword, Gram chopped Gothorn in half.

Sigurd died a few moments later with his three-year-old son, Sigmund. Brynhild then killed herself with her sword. She was burned with Sigurd.

Gunnar and Hogni took Sigurd's wealth with the cursed ring Andvarinaut and ruled over the land.

King Atli Brynhild's brother then married Gudrun and, together, they had children. Once, King Atli invited the two brothers, Gunnar and Hogni, to come and visit, and they both accepted the invitation.

Before the two brothers left home, they hid their gold on the river called the Rhine.

When the brothers arrived at Atli's Kingdom, his men attacked and captured them. King Atli ripped out Hogni's heart with a knife while he was still alive. Gunnar was thrown down into a snake pit. He was bitten just below the breastbone and died.

After Gudrun killed the two sons, she had two goblets made from the skulls, using gold and silver. During a funeral feast for the two brothers, Gudrun served mead mixed with their blood to King Arti in these two skull cups.

Gudrun also roasted the hearts of the two brothers and served them to the King. After he had eaten the two hearts and drunk the mead, she told him what she had done.

In the evening, when people at the feast had fallen asleep, Gudrun came into the hall and killed the king in his chair. Later set fire to the hall and everyone inside burned to death.

Gudrun then walked down to the river and wanted to drown herself. However, the waves carried her to the lands ruled by King Jonak.

When the King saw how beautiful Gudrun was, he married her, and together, they had three sons: Sorli, Hamdir, and Erp.

In the meantime, King Jormunrek the Powerful had heard about the beauty of Svanhild (Sigurd's daughter), so he sent his son Randver to ask for her hand.

When Randver arrived at Jonak, he was given permission to bring Svanhild back to Jormunrek.

Bikki, the king's adviser, said that it would be better if Randver married Svanhild instead of the king.

Both Randver and Svanhild liked this idea and married. However, when King Jormunrek heard about it, he hanged his son and his men rode down Svanhild, trampling her to death under the feet of their horses.

When Gudrun learned about this, she sought vengeance for Svanhild and told her sons to kill the king. Sorli and Hamdir were to chop off his arms and legs and Erp was to behead him.

Sorli and Hamdir asked Erp what assistance they could expect from him. Erp said, "I can help you, just like the hand helps the foot."

However, Sorli and Hamdir answered back, saying that the foot is not supported at all by the hand. They killed him because Erp was the son whom Gudrun loved most.

In the evening, the brothers arrived at King Jormunrek's sleeping quarters. As they struck off his hands and legs, he awoke and called out to his guards, asking for help.

Then Hamdir said, "If we had left Erp alive, the head would have been cut, so the king would not have been able to call for his guards."

The guards arrived in the room and attacked the two brothers. However, they could not attack them with their weapons, so Odin appeared as an old one-eyed man and used stones instead of swords. The guards picked up the stones and threw them at the brothers until they fell.

Later, the King bled out, leaving the house of Gjuki without any descendants.

CONCLUSION

I hope that you have enjoyed reading this introduction to Scandinavian mythology and that you now have a better understanding of the Vikings—in particular, their myths and legends. This is the first in a series of books that will discuss the myths and legends of various cultures, so please stay tuned for information about future releases.

Printed in Great Britain
by Amazon

61075745R00078